The Bargain Bride

"You will be my wife, and I have chosen the gown you will wear!"

Aleda resented the authoritative way Mr. Winton spoke, and looking at him with a hatred she could not suppress, she asked:

"And if I disobey your august command?"

There was a twist to Mr. Winton's lips before he replied:

"In which case, you will find I am a very experienced maid!"

For a moment Aleda could hardly believe he meant what he said, until despite herself the colour rose in her cheeks. . . .

A Camfield Novel of Love
by Barbara Cartland

———

"Barbara Cartland's novels are all distinguished by their intelligence, good sense, and good nature..."
— ROMANTIC TIMES

"Who could give better advice on how to keep your romance going strong than the world's most famous romance novelist, Barbara Cartland?"
— THE STAR

Camfield Place,
Hatfield
Hertfordshire,
England

Dearest Reader,

Camfield Novels of Love mark a very exciting era of my books with Jove. They have already published nearly two hundred of my titles since they became my first publisher in America, and now all my original paperback romances in the future will be published exclusively by them.

As you already know, Camfield Place in Hertfordshire is my home, which originally existed in 1275, but was rebuilt in 1867 by the grandfather of Beatrix Potter.

It was here in this lovely house, with the best view in the county, that she wrote *The Tale of Peter Rabbit*. Mr. McGregor's garden is exactly as she described it. The door in the wall that the fat little rabbit could not squeeze underneath and the goldfish pool where the white cat sat twitching its tail are still there.

I had Camfield Place blessed when I came here in 1950 and was so happy with my husband until he died, and now with my children and grandchildren, that I know the atmosphere is filled with love and we have all been very lucky.

It is easy here to write of love and I know you will enjoy the Camfield Novels of Love. Their plots are definitely exciting and the covers very romantic. They come to you, like all my books, with love.

Bless you,

CAMFIELD NOVELS OF LOVE

by Barbara Cartland

THE POOR GOVERNESS
WINGED VICTORY
LUCKY IN LOVE
LOVE AND THE MARQUIS
A MIRACLE IN MUSIC
LIGHT OF THE GODS
BRIDE TO A BRIGAND
LOVE COMES WEST
A WITCH'S SPELL
SECRETS
THE STORMS OF LOVE
MOONLIGHT ON THE
  SPHINX
WHITE LILAC
REVENGE OF THE HEART
THE ISLAND OF LOVE
THERESA AND A TIGER
LOVE IS HEAVEN
MIRACLE FOR A MADONNA
A VERY UNUSUAL WIFE
THE PERIL AND THE
  PRINCE
ALONE AND AFRAID
TEMPTATION OF A
  TEACHER
ROYAL PUNISHMENT
THE DEVILISH DECEPTION

PARADISE FOUND
LOVE IS A GAMBLE
A VICTORY FOR LOVE
LOOK WITH LOVE
NEVER FORGET LOVE
HELGA IN HIDING
SAFE AT LAST
HAUNTED
CROWNED WITH LOVE
ESCAPE
THE DEVIL DEFEATED
THE SECRET OF THE
  MOSQUE
A DREAM IN SPAIN
THE LOVE TRAP
LISTEN TO LOVE
THE GOLDEN CAGE
LOVE CASTS OUT FEAR
A WORLD OF LOVE
DANCING ON A RAINBOW
LOVE JOINS THE CLANS
AN ANGEL RUNS AWAY
FORCED TO MARRY
BEWILDERED IN BERLIN
WANTED—A WEDDING
  RING
THE EARL ESCAPES

STARLIGHT OVER TUNIS
THE LOVE PUZZLE
LOVE AND KISSES
SAPPHIRES IN SIAM
A CARETAKER OF LOVE
SECRETS OF THE HEART
RIDING IN THE SKY
LOVERS IN LISBON
LOVE IS INVINCIBLE
THE GODDESS OF LOVE
AN ADVENTURE OF LOVE
THE HERB FOR HAPPINESS
ONLY A DREAM
SAVED BY LOVE
LITTLE TONGUES OF FIRE
A CHIEFTAIN FINDS LOVE
THE LOVELY LIAR
THE PERFUME OF THE GODS
A KNIGHT IN PARIS
REVENGE IS SWEET
THE PASSIONATE PRINCESS
SOLITA AND THE SPIES
THE PERFECT PEARL
LOVE IS A MAZE
A CIRCUS FOR LOVE
THE TEMPLE OF LOVE
THE BARGAIN BRIDE

Other books by Barbara Cartland

THE ADVENTURER
AGAIN THIS RAPTURE
BARBARA CARTLAND'S
  BOOK OF BEAUTY
  AND HEALTH
BLUE-HEATHER
BROKEN BARRIERS
THE CAPTIVE HEART
THE COIN OF LOVE
THE COMPLACENT WIFE
COUNT THE STARS
DESIRE OF THE HEART
DESPERATE DEFIANCE
THE DREAM WITHIN
ELIZABETHAN LOVER
THE ENCHANTING EVIL
ESCAPE FROM PASSION
FOR ALL ETERNITY
A GOLDEN GONDOLA
A HAZARD OF HEARTS
A HEART IS BROKEN
THE HIDDEN HEART
THE HORIZONS OF LOVE
IN THE ARMS OF LOVE
THE IRRESISTIBLE BUCK

THE KISS OF PARIS
THE KISS OF THE DEVIL
A KISS OF SILK
THE KNAVE OF HEARTS
THE LEAPING FLAME
A LIGHT TO THE HEART
LIGHTS OF LOVE
THE LITTLE PRETENDER
LOST ENCHANTMENT
LOVE AT FORTY
LOVE FORBIDDEN
LOVE IN HIDING
LOVE IS THE ENEMY
LOVE ME FOREVER
LOVE TO THE RESCUE
LOVE UNDER FIRE
THE MAGIC OF HONEY
METTERNICH THE
  PASSIONATE
  DIPLOMAT
MONEY, MAGIC AND
  MARRIAGE
NO HEART IS FREE
THE ODIOUS DUKE
OPEN WINGS

A RAINBOW TO HEAVEN
THE RELUCTANT BRIDE
THE SCANDALOUS LIFE
  OF KING CAROL
THE SECRET FEAR
THE SMUGGLED
  HEART
A SONG OF LOVE
STARS IN MY HEART
STOLEN HALO
SWEET ENCHANTRESS
SWEET PUNISHMENT
THEFT OF A HEART
THE THIEF OF LOVE
THIS TIME IT'S LOVE
TOUCH A STAR
TOWARDS THE STARS
THE UNKNOWN HEART
WE DANCED ALL NIGHT
THE WINGS OF ECSTASY
THE WINGS OF LOVE
WINGS ON MY HEART
WOMAN, THE ENIGMA

A NEW CAMFIELD NOVEL OF LOVE BY

BARBARA CARTLAND

The Bargain Bride

JOVE BOOKS, NEW YORK

THE BARGAIN BRIDE

A Jove Book/published by arrangement with
the author

PRINTING HISTORY
Jove edition/December 1989

ISBN: 0-515-10198-2

Jove Books are published by The Berkley Publishing Group,
200 Madison Avenue, New York, New York 10016.
The name "JOVE" and the "J" logo
are trademarks belonging to Jove Publications, Inc.

PRINTED IN THE UNITED STATES OF AMERICA

10 9 8 7 6 5 4 3 2 1

AUTHOR'S NOTE

THE young Bucks and Beaux of the Regency had not enough to do and therefore spent their time gambling, drinking and chasing pretty "Cyprians" who made the most of the situation.

There were Gambling Houses all over London and all the Clubs had Card-Rooms, where their members played for very high stakes.

London was an obvious temptation to any young man as soon as the war was over and he returned to civilian life after suffering the hardships he had endured in Wellington's Army.

Many of the aristocrats gambled away not only the treasures which were not entailed in their ancestral houses, but also property, including Streets and Squares in London which today would fetch astronomical figures.

It was difficult not to feel sorry for them in that they were not only foolish and foolhardy, but they also had a pride which carried them through every situation, even when they became bankrupt.

The reverence shown in this book by the Chinese for their ancient relics continues to this day, and a sacred carving handed down from father to son is worshipped by every member of his family and all his household.

chapter one

1818

THE members of Whites Club sitting in the Morning-Room looked up in surprise as the Earl of Blakeney burst through the door.

"For God's sake, give me a drink!" he said to one of the Club Servants.

Seeing Lord Fulbourne on the other side of the room, he flung himself down in one of the leather chairs beside him.

"I am finished, Charles," he said, "completely and absolutely finished!"

"I presume," Charles Fulbourne answered, "that you have lost your money."

"I have lost all I own and a damned sight more besides!" the Earl replied. "Unless somebody is ready to bail me out, the next time you see me will be in the Fleet!"

Lord Fulbourne looked at him in surprise.

The way his friend was speaking made it sound as if his reference to the Fleet Prison was not a joke, but a reality.

"How can you have been such a fool," he asked in a lowered voice because he realised the whole room was listening, "as to play when you know you cannot afford it?"

"It was my only chance to pay off some of my creditors, but now Cayton can whistle for his money. You cannot get blood from a stone!"

As if the mention of his name conjured him up, Lord Anthony Cayton, a tall, good-looking young man, came into the room.

He glanced around, saw the Earl, and walked towards him.

"If you think you are going to get away without paying me, Blakeney," he said angrily, "you are mistaken! You have welshed on me before, but this time I will have you thrown out of the Club!"

"I will throw myself out!" the Earl retorted.

He rose from his chair as he spoke, and confronted Lord Anthony. The two young men glared at each other like ferocious beasts.

There was a faint smile on the faces of some of those listening. They knew that the Earl and Lord Anthony had quarrelled a fortnight ago over the possession of a very pretty "Cyprian."

That the Earl had won had infuriated Lord Anthony, who had sworn his revenge.

It did not appease him when he learned that, finding the Earl's pockets were "to let," the Cyprian had left him within a week for a rich Protector.

"I am going to call you out," Lord Anthony said now, aggressively.

"You can call until you are blue in the face," the Earl retorted, "I am going to the country to see if I have anything saleable left. But I promise you that any pickings that remain after the tradesmen have got their hands on it will be 'chicken-feed'!"

"If you say much more," Lord Anthony replied, "I will knock you down!"

As it seemed that was exactly what he intended, Lord Fulbourne rose to stand between them, saying:

"Stop it, you two! You know as well as I do, Anthony, that David has not a penny to his name!"

He turned to the Earl and went on:

"And you, David, have no right to gamble when you are well aware your house is falling around your ears, and those who rely on you have not enough to eat."

The way he spoke made the Earl look slightly shame-faced.

Lord Anthony turned on his heel and, muttering beneath his breath, walked out of the Morning-Room.

Lord Fulbourne put his hand on the Earl's arm.

"Go home, David," he said in a quiet voice. "I have a feeling things are more desperate than you realise."

"I know how desperate they are," the Earl replied, "and the best thing I can do is to blow a piece of lead through my head!"

He left as he spoke, and there was a buzz of voices as the members, who had been stunned into silence by the drama taking place in front of them, began to discuss it.

Lord Fulbourne sat down again and, as he did so, a man rose from a chair in the corner where he had

3

been reading *The Times* and sat down next to him.

"My name is Winton," he said. "I knew your father. I have only just returned to England and I am curious to know what all this fuss is about."

Lord Fulbourne looked round and realised the man was someone he had never seen before.

He guessed he was about thirty-four years of age, and had a distinct presence which gave him an air of authority.

He was also handsome with a square chin. But Lord Fulbourne thought there was something hard about his eyes and the firmness of his mouth.

It was an arresting face, and he wondered who the newcomer was and how he had become a member of Whites.

The most exclusive Club, and one of the oldest in London, it was noted for having as its members only the most blue-blooded aristocrats.

It was also harder to get elected to Whites than to any other Club in St. James's.

Because the man opposite him was waiting for an answer to his question, Lord Fulbourne said:

"You heard the Earl of Blakeney is 'below hatches,' and that is unfortunately the truth. He inherited a large amount of debts when his father died, and has managed to exist by selling anything that was saleable from his ancestral home."

He realised that Mr. Winton, if that was his real name, was listening intently, and he added:

"I believe his debts have reached such proportions that the tradesmen are forcing the sale of everything that is left."

"And if he cannot pay them?" the man called

Winton asked, "does it really mean he will go to prison?"

"It is certainly a possibility," Charles Fulbourne admitted. "The tradesmen are tired of Gentlemen who live on credit, and he was informed a week ago that they intend to take action against him and show him up as an example to other young men who are so irresponsible."

Mr. Winton was silent for a moment before he said:

"I think I remember the late Earl."

"Everybody was very fond of him," Lord Fulbourne remarked, "but he was a gambler, and his children have to suffer the consequences."

"His—children?" Mr. Winton questioned.

"David has a sister," Lord Fulbourne replied, "who, if she could have a Season in London, would undoubtedly be an 'Incomparable.'"

He paused before he continued, as if choosing his words:

"She is very lovely, in fact 'beautiful' is the right word, but, unlike her brother, she is too proud to take what she cannot pay for. She therefore stays in the country."

"A sad story," Mr. Winton said, "and I think I am right in saying that the Earl of Blakeney's house is in Hertfordshire."

"Blake Hall is only about fifteen to twenty miles from here," Lord Fulbourne answered, "and it is there the tradesmen intend to confront him with their bills."

He sighed before he added:

"I suppose those of us who can afford it must turn

up and buy something we do not want, just for friendship's sake."

His reluctance to do anything of the kind was very obvious, and Mr. Winton gave him a penetrating look before he said:

"It is always interesting in such circumstances for a man to see how many real friends he has."

There was no doubt that he was speaking cynically.

He rose to his feet as he spoke and walked back to the chair he had vacated in a corner of the Morning-Room.

* * *

It was late in the afternoon when, driving in a Phaeton he had not paid for, with horses he had borrowed from a friend, the Earl of Blakeney arrived back at Blake Hall.

When he drove in through the gates that needed painting, past lodges that were empty with their windows boarded up, there was a despairing expression on his face.

As the house came in sight at the end of the drive, it looked, with its mellow bricks which had become a pale pink over the years, very beautiful.

But as he drew nearer he could see the broken windows which had not been repaired, and the tiles which had fallen from the roof.

Moss and grass were growing in the cracks in the steps leading up to the front door.

As the Earl drew his horses to a standstill, he shouted at the top of his voice.

It was a sound which echoed round the house until it reached the stables.

An old man with white hair appeared slowly round the corner, and it took him, the Earl thought, an inordinate amount of time to reach the horses' heads.

"Oi weren't expectin' ye, M'Lord," he said in a croaking voice.

"I was not expecting to come!" the Earl replied sharply as he stepped down from the Phaeton. "Put the horses in the stable, Glover. They will be collected tomorrow."

"Very good, M'Lord," Glover replied.

He was grumbling beneath his breath as he led the horses away towards the stable.

The Earl walked in through the front door, which was open.

The hall, with its dark oak panelling, was too familiar for him to notice the dust on the floor, or that the diamond-paned windows which bore the heraldic coat-of-arms of the Blakeneys were both dirty and cracked.

He threw his high hat down on a table that needed polishing and again shouted at the top of his voice:

"Aleda! Aleda!"

There was no reply, and he was just about to shout again when there was the sound of footsteps.

A moment later his sister came running into the hall.

"David!" she exclaimed. "I was not expecting you!"

Her brother did not reply, and, standing in front of him as she looked up into his face, she said:

"What has . . . happened? What is . . . worrying you?"

"Everything!" the Earl answered. "Is there anything to drink in this dungheap?"

"There is water, or there may be a few coffee-beans left."

The Earl made a sound of disgust and walked across the hall and opened the door of the Drawing Room.

It was beautifully proportioned with windows looking out on what had once been the rose-garden.

The furniture, however, was sparse.

There were marks on the walls where the pictures had been removed, and what had obviously been a mirror was gone from the mantelshelf.

Also missing were the Dresden china figures and the Sèvres clock which the Earl remembered as a child.

He turned round to stand with his back to the empty fireplace in which the brass fire-irons had not been polished, nor was the fire-basket blackened.

His sister followed him into the room and now she said apprehensively.

"You had better . . . tell me . . . the worst . . . David!"

"Very well," her brother replied, "my creditors are coming here tomorrow to demand that we sell everything that is left in the house, and thinking they can find a fool to buy the house itself!"

Aleda gave a little cry of horror.

"Surely you . . . cannot mean . . . that?"

Her brother did not answer, and after a moment she said:

"I always . . . believed the house was . . . entailed so that it . . . could not be . . . sold."

"That is what Papa believed," the Earl replied,

"but actually, the 'entailment,' or whatever the thing is called, lapsed after the seventh Earl died without having a son, and, although a cousin inherited, he was not in direct male line. That broke the entail."

"I had no . . . idea of . . . that," Aleda said in a low voice.

"If Papa had known it, I am certain he would have sold the house lock, stock, and barrel!" the Earl said sharply. "And now that is what I have to do."

His voice was bitter as he continued:

"I cannot imagine we will get anything for the mess it is in at the moment, and after the war, nobody seems to have much money."

"But, David . . . what are . . . you going to . . . do?" Aleda asked in a frightened voice.

"If the tradesmen have their way, I shall go to prison!"

She gave a cry of horror.

"Oh . . . no . . . not . . . that!"

"They are determined to make an example of someone who they consider has defaulted on them."

"Then . . . what can . . . we do?" Aleda asked.

"I have not the slightest idea," her brother replied, "and you know as well as I do, Aleda, there is nothing worth sixpence in the house, or I should have sold it long ago!"

"But we must . . . have a . . . roof over . . . our heads!" Aleda cried.

"I expect there is a cottage empty somewhere on the estate," the Earl said thoughtfully, "but as you know already, they are in a worse state than the house!"

They looked at each other for a moment.

9

"When I am in prison," the Earl replied, "you will just have to camp here on your own."

"That is . . . what I am doing . . . anyway," Aleda answered. "There is only old Betsy left . . . who has nowhere to go . . . and Glover, who is . . . terrified of being . . . taken to the . . . Workhouse."

The Earl threw himself down on a sofa, which had not been sold because it had a leg broken and was propped up on a couple of bricks.

There was silence until he saw the expression on his sister's face and said in a different tone from what he had used before:

"I am sorry, Aleda. I know I have made a damned fool of myself, but it is too late now to put the clock back."

His sister sat down beside him and put her hand over his.

"I understand, Dearest, that after the war, you wanted to enjoy yourself."

"I do not suppose my activities would have made much difference to the position in which we find ourselves," the Earl said, "and now we have to face facts. If I go to prison, you will starve, unless somebody looks after you."

"There is only one person who wishes to do that," Aleda said.

"I suppose you mean Shuttle!"

"He called on me yesterday and offered me a house in London, diamonds, and a carriage of my own!"

"Curse his damned impertinence!" the Earl swore. "How dare he insult you?"

"It is hardly an insult," Aleda said in a low voice, "when he realised I was hungry, and, because I was

10

not expecting him, my gown was in tatters."

The Earl looked at her sharply.

"You are thinking of accepting his proposition?"

"I would rather die first!"

As she spoke, her voice seemed to ring out.

"He has a wife and children, and everything he does and says makes me feel sick!"

She rose from the sofa and walked across the room to the window.

"I hate him!" she said. "I hate all men. . . . At the same time . . . I am . . . frightened!"

"So am I!" the Earl admitted.

Aleda looked out at the sunshine, which somehow contrived to make the overgrown flowers, the creepers, and even the weeds look attractive.

"I was thinking this morning," she remarked, "that we have but one thing left."

"And what is that?" her brother enquired.

"Our pride," Aleda said. "Whatever happens to us, we are Blakes! Our ancestors fought at the Battle of Agincourt. They were Royalists who died at the hands of Oliver Cromwell, and our grandfather was one of the best Generals in Marlborough's Army."

"A fat lot of good that does us now!" the Earl said disparagingly.

"They fought for their lives as we have to fight for ours," Aleda said, "and why should we be . . . defeated by our . . . debts?"

She paused as if she expected her brother to say something, and when he was silent she went on:

"Somehow I feel that however bad everything seems, the ghosts of those who have lived in this house are still fighting beside us. When they died . . . the family survived . . . and so must we."

As she finished speaking, the Earl rose from the sofa and walked towards her.

He put his arms around her waist, then, as she moved a little nearer to him, he said:

"Tell me what to do, Aleda."

It was the cry of a small boy who was frightened of the dark, and Aleda said:

"Whatever happens, we will face them with our chins high and, if you like, defiantly. Even if they take everything we possess, we will still be alive!"

She thought as she spoke that they were already very near to starvation.

For the last month, while her brother had been in London, it was only because Glover had managed to snare a few rabbits that they had anything to eat.

There had been pigeons and the occasional duck or game bird until the gunpowder ran out and they had been unable to afford to buy any more.

There were still a few vegetables in the garden to go with the rabbits.

"You are very brave, Aleda," the Earl said, "and I only hope that I shall live up to your expectations."

"Just remember that you are a Blake," Aleda said, "and when these people come ... they will see for themselves ... the position we are ... in."

The Earl did not speak, but she knew he was thinking that the shopkeepers would not go back to London empty-handed.

They would take him with them.

He would rot in the Fleet Prison unless by a miracle somebody bought the house and the estate at a price which was enough to let him free.

"The best thing I could do," he said aloud, "is to put a bullet through my head."

Aleda turned on him angrily:

"That would be a cowardly thing to do."

There was a little sob in her voice as she went on:

"You are all the family I have left. Our relatives never approved of Papa . . . and they do not . . . approve of . . . you. We have to support each other . . . David . . . and I . . . cannot be . . . alone."

The Earl drew in his breath.

"There must be someone besides that swine Shuttle!"

Aleda laughed.

"Do you really think there is any chance of me meeting men here? I could hardly invite them to the house when we cannot afford any sort of hospitality."

"Now you are making me feel ashamed," the Earl protested. "I know I have been ungrateful and selfish, and I should have thought of you instead of enjoying myself in London."

"I understood," Aleda said, "and when you came back after the war . . . I was . . . only seventeen."

"Now you are nearly nineteen," the Earl remarked, "and you are lovely, Aleda! If I could have taken you to London, I know you would have had a dozen proposals of marriage!"

"That is the last thing I want," Aleda said. "I have told you . . . I hate men. If only we had a little money . . . I would be completely happy here with the . . . horses and dogs."

"You are talking like that only because of Shuttle's dirty suggestions," her brother said angrily. "How did he ever get to meet you in the first place?"

Aleda gave a little laugh.

"He was out hunting and his horse cast a shoe, and seeing how impressive Blake Hall looked from a distance, he came to see if we employed a black-smith."

The Earl laughed as if he could not help it.

"It must have given him a surprise when he saw that the stables were falling to the ground!"

"He saw me!" Aleda corrected her brother. "And that was enough! Ever since, he has not left me alone and I have to hide every time I see him . . . coming up . . . the drive!"

"Curse him! I should have thrown him out a long time ago!"

"At first you welcomed the wine he brought you."

"I had no idea he was asking you to be his mistress!"

"There is nothing else he can offer me, but if he were a widower, I would still not accept his money . . . or him! I hate . . . him! He makes me creep . . . and the last present he . . . gave me I threw into the back of his . . . carriage as he . . . drove away."

"What was it?" the Earl asked.

"A diamond bracelet, I think, from what he said, but I did not open the case!"

She knew without saying anything that her brother was thinking that the diamonds would have at least paid off some of his debts.

"Remember you are a Blake," she said sharply, "and if we go down . . . we go down with all flags flying and our . . . heads . . . unbowed!"

*　　*　　*

Later in the evening, after they had eaten a frugal meal of rabbit with a few vegetables, Aleda made the Earl open up the Banqueting Hall.

They arranged the few chairs that were left at the end of it under the Minstrels' Gallery.

"We will receive our guests here," she said, "and you will tell them exactly the position we are in."

She saw her brother was about to refuse, and she said:

"You are not to be humble, merely frank and honest."

"Why should I be that?" the Earl asked sullenly.

"Because there is no point in being rude or secretive," Aleda said. "Be frank and you should also say that you are sorry that you are so much in their debt! If you are pleasant, they might not be so vindictive as to send you to prison."

She knew the Earl was not convinced, and went on:

"We have nothing to lose by being polite, and you will certainly not find work if you are behind bars."

"Work!" the Earl exclaimed. "What do you mean —work?"

"There must be something you can do," Aleda said. "Have you ever thought of counting your talents?"

"I have none."

"That is nonsense! We all have talents of some sort. I have been trying to think how saleable mine are."

"Saleable?" the Earl questioned suspiciously.

"Not to some man who wants me only for my pretty face!" Aleda snapped. "I was thinking I might become a teacher of some sort. I have been fairly well educated, I can play the piano, I can paint in water colours, and, of course, I can ride."

She gave a little cry.

"That is what you can do, David!"

"Ride? Of course I can ride! What do you mean?"

"I remember how you told me that the Duke of Wellington was very impressed when you won the Steeple Chase he had arranged for the Officers in the Army of Occupation."

"That is true," the Earl replied, "but I cannot see how I can make money like that."

"Supposing we persuaded one of your friends to help you?" Aleda said. "If you could break in horses which you bought cheap, then you could sell them for perhaps a good sum."

For a moment her brother's face seemed to lighten. Then he answered:

"I hardly think what we will get for selling one horse, or half-a-dozen, will do more than pay for our food. It would be a mere 'drop in the ocean' compared to what I owe!"

Aleda bit back the words that came to her lips, and after a moment she said gently:

"We have to show the people who are prosecuting you that you are ... prepared to ... try to pay your ... debts."

"Very well, have it your own way! I can only hope that by some extraordinary stroke of luck we may be successful."

He did not sound very hopeful.

Later, when she was in bed in the darkness, Aleda admitted to herself that it was very unlikely that the tradesmen would listen, or that anybody would provide David with a horse to break in.

She was well aware that he had already borrowed from his friends while he had been in London.

He had stayed with them, he had ridden their horses and driven their Phaetons.

He had also, she was sure, taken money from them and expended every penny of it in what she could describe to herself only as "riotous living."

She had no idea exactly what this meant, but she was quite sure that David had drunk much more than was good for him.

She thought, too, that he must have spent a great deal of his time with the sort of women of whom her mother would not have approved.

And yet it was her mother, and her father, for that matter, who had spoilt David ever since he was born.

For some unknown reason for which the doctors had no explanation, the ninth Earl of Blakeney and his wife had been married for fifteen years before, to their astonishment and joy, they produced a son.

Because David was so good-looking and they were so thrilled to have him, he had ruled the household from his cot.

It was inevitable, therefore, that he should think that the whole world was there for him to walk on.

The Earl and Countess had once again been delighted when, four years later, they had had a daughter.

Aleda, as soon as she was old enough, realised that David was the light of their lives.

Although they loved her, she was a very poor second to her brother.

She, too, loved David; it was impossible not to.

He was impulsive, selfish, and yet at the same time he was courageous, kind-hearted, and in many ways very intelligent.

He had gone from Eton, where he had been educated, straight into the Army.

He had been commended twice by the Duke of Wellington for Gallantry and at the end of the war had received a medal.

He was one of the Officers who the Great Duke insisted should be with him in the Army of Occupation.

It was only when he resigned his commission and came back to England that he began to realise that, to the Earl of Blakeney, London was an alluring place.

He had a position in the Social World, and he was the envy of many of his brother officers.

It was inevitable that it should go to his head, and he completely forgot the way that his estate had gone to rack and ruin despite his father's efforts to keep it going.

His sister had become nothing more than a slave in a house that was falling down.

Now he was faced with reality, and Aleda knew that she had to comfort and sustain him as her mother would have done if she were alive.

"It is not going to be easy, Mama," she said in the darkness, "but I am praying desperately hard that David will not be sent to prison. Please help me . . . help us both. I cannot believe that . . . you and Papa are not . . . worried . . . about us."

She felt as if her prayer moved from her heart to her lips, and up into the sky.

Somehow, although she had no real reason for thinking so, she fell asleep thinking that her mother had heard her.

* * *

When morning came Aleda went down early.

She found, after searching amongst the weeds and grasses in what had once been the chicken-run, that one of the old hens that was still there had laid an egg.

She carried it carefully back to the house and gave it to David when he came down for breakfast.

She thought that despite their worries, he was looking brighter and certainly better than he had yesterday.

She knew, if the truth was told, it was because he had had nothing to drink at their frugal dinner.

The amount of claret and brandy he drank when he was in London was bad for him.

She gave him the egg and the toast she had made from the bread she had received from the Baker in exchange for a rabbit which Glover had snared for her.

There was no butter, but one of the cottagers who knew, as did the rest of the village, the state she was in, had given her a comb of honey from his beehive.

She had been using it sparingly so that there was enough both for David and herself.

Yet she was wondering despairingly what they would have tomorrow, when David said:

"I must say, I still feel hungry!"

"Perhaps some of your friends who are coming from London to take part in the sale will bring something substantial with them," Aleda suggested.

She laughed before she added:

"A leg of lamb or a boar's head would, I assure you, be far more welcome than a case of wine."

"I want both!" David replied.

"Then, as Mama used to say," Aleda replied, "'Want must be your master'!"

"If you ask me, he is a very hard taskmaster!"

They laughed because it sounded so ridiculous; then, as if he suddenly noticed her for the first time, David exclaimed:

"You are looking very smart!"

"It is the last of Mama's gowns," Aleda explained. "I have been very careful with them, but unless I was to go naked, I had to wear something. But I kept this one for special occasions."

"I suppose you think this is special!" David said bitterly.

"It is to me," Aleda replied. "Now go and put on your smartest coat, tie your cravat in a 'Mathematical,' which I am told is the very latest style in St. James's."

"Who on earth told you that?" David asked.

"Glover, whose son came to see him last week. He is working as valet to the Duke of Northumberland, who, I am assured, is very much 'up to scratch.'"

"You really should not talk to servants," the Earl said.

"Then who else?" Aleda enquired. "It is more eloquent than the croaking of frogs and the caws of the rooks!"

Again David had the grace to look shamefaced.

"I swear," he said, "that if we have a penny left over after the devouring wolves have left, I am spending it on you!"

He spoke anxiously, and Aleda rose to drop him a curtsy.

"Thank you kindly, Sir," she said, "but I am not

counting my pennies until I hear them tinkle."

It was impossible for the Earl not to laugh.

Then because time was passing and they were not certain at what hour the tradesmen would appear, they both went upstairs.

Aleda had polished David's Hessian boots the previous night, before she went to bed.

She had also pressed several white cravats in case he should spoil one.

In her own room there was a bonnet which went with her mother's gown.

It was fortunate that the fashion had not altered much since the Countess's death five years before.

The gown, which was of blue gauze, the colour of her eyes and Aleda's, had small puffed sleeves, a high waist, and was decorated with frills and ruching around the hem.

Mother and daughter had more or less the same figure.

The blue of the gown made Aleda's skin seem very white and her hair the soft gold of the dawn.

There was no doubt, if there had been anyone to notice her, that she was lovely in the tradition of the Madonna painted by Botticelli.

There was something humanly captivating, and at the same time spiritually beautiful, in her face which was not found among the Beauties that were acclaimed as "Incomparables" in the *Beau Ton*.

When she lifted the high-crowned bonnet to put it on her head, she thought it was not grand enough.

Leaving her bedroom, she went to the one opposite that had been her mother's and found in the wardrobe two others.

One of them was decorated with flowers, the other with ostrich feathers.

She added these to the ribbons that had been skilfully arranged on the bonnet which matched her gown.

It made her look, she thought, certainly striking, and very much more flamboyant.

As she came from her bedroom, her brother appeared from his.

For a moment he just stared at her. Then he laughed.

"You will certainly surprise them!"

"That is what I want to do," Aleda replied, "and David, you look a complete 'Tulip of Fashion.'"

"If you call me that, Aleda, I shall consider myself insulted!" David said. "And I shall take off my coat and greet them in my shirt-sleeves! Preferably one that has holes in it!"

He was only teasing her, but Aleda said:

"Please think of your speech, and remember how important it is for both of us."

"I have not forgotten," David replied.

They walked together to the top of the stairs.

Aleda had left the door open. She had also brushed away some of the accumulation of dust, and arranged a bowl of roses on a table near the fireplace.

She was, however, as they began to descend the stairs, acutely conscious that the huge grandfather clock she had loved had gone.

So had the barometer she had loved as a child, which was a hundred years old.

The large armchairs with their carved backs were missing, and the Persian rug which had lain in front of the fireplace was no longer there.

'There is nothing to sell,' she thought with a sense of panic, 'except the staircase and the panelling.'

Then as she walked down, keeping pace with David, she saw through the open door the horses of a large carriage coming up the drive.

chapter two

THE occupants of the first vehicle came walking up the front steps.

As they did so, Aleda was aware that they were sniggering and laughing amongst themselves at the dilapidated condition of the house.

At the same time, as they entered the hall she thought they were slightly awed, and she was certain that they had never entered an ancestral home before.

It was obvious they had not expected to be received by the Earl and herself.

Standing against the marble mantelpiece they looked, she hoped, impressive.

"How do you do, Carter?" the Earl said to his Coach-builder, the first man to approach him.

He held out his hand, and there was a distinct hesitation before the man took it; he was obviously somewhat flustered at the sight of Aleda.

"If you go straight down the passage," she said, "you will find everything arranged for you in the Banqueting Hall."

It was a sentence she was to repeat a large number of times before there was a pause and she thought perhaps nobody else was arriving.

Then, looking through the open door, she was aware that a very smart Phaeton had drawn up outside.

She knew from the expression on her brother's face that they were his friends from London.

She knew it upset him that they should see him humiliated by the tradesmen, and she said quickly:

"It was kind of them to come, and I am sure they will buy something, and you must not forget that we need the money."

He gave her a wry smile to show he understood what she was saying.

Then Lord Fulbourne and two other members of Whites came through the door.

"How are you, Blakeney?" they asked genially. "We thought we would come to support you. We are well aware it might be our turn tomorrow!"

"It is jolly decent of you," the Earl answered, "and let me introduce you to my sister."

Aleda was aware that Lord Fulbourne's eyes were very complimentary, as were those of the two men who followed him.

She directed them to the Banqueting Hall and was not surprised when later she went there to find they were sitting in the front seats as if by right.

The tradesmen sat as far to the back as possible.

She and the Earl had collected every chair in the

house, thinking it would be better for those harassing him to sit rather than stand.

There were still other carriages coming up the drive, and when finally there were no more, Aleda thought there must be at least fifty people waiting for them in the Banqueting Hall.

"There will be no more," she said to the Earl.

"I hope you are right," he replied. "I have no idea who half of them are."

"I think some are just sightseers," Aleda said soothingly. "There are always tattle-tongues who want to be in on the act."

"What you should really say is 'in at the kill'!" her brother said gloomily.

She slipped her arm through his.

"Keep your chin up," she said, "I cannot bear to see you grovelling."

"I am damned if I will do that!" he said violently.

She knew she had succeeded in putting him on his mettle, and they walked quite jauntily down the passage and into the Banqueting Hall.

Just as they reached it she was aware there was somebody behind them; she thought another carriage must have arrived somewhat belatedly.

Yet she also thought it would be a mistake to wait any longer, and walked into the Banqueting Hall ahead of her brother.

They stood under the Minstrels' Gallery, and there was a small table in front of them on which, quite unnecessarily, Aleda had put a few papers.

She thought it looked more businesslike and it also, in some way she did not like to think about, protected David from those in front of him.

When she looked around she thought, with the

exception of his three friends in the front row, the tradesmen looked surly and frightening.

She knew they had combined as a gang to attack her brother.

She was sure they would not wish to return to London empty-handed and to all intents and purposes defeated.

"Please . . . God . . . help us," she prayed, and thought she was only a lone voice crying in the wilderness.

With commendable self-assurance, the Earl stood in front of the table while Aleda sat down beside him.

"I would like," he began, "to have welcomed you to my home, instead of which I feel I must apologise that you have felt obliged to come here to alert me to my responsibilities, of which I am well aware.

"Now you have seen the house and the state it is in, your eyes will tell you very much better than I can that there is very little to sell, and I can only hope that some gentleman here will purchase the whole estate so that you can divide the money between you."

There was a little murmur at this amongst the tradesmen listening.

Because David looked so handsome and spoke so clearly and sincerely, Aleda could only hope that they were impressed.

"What I am going to do," the Earl went on, "is first to inform you of what I do possess in the way of buildings, acreage, and, of course, the house itself."

He brought a piece of paper from his pocket which he had prepared with some difficulty, hoping to make what he possessed sound more attractive than it actually was.

His thousand acres could hardly be described as being in "good heart," considering it had not been farmed for several years.

The farms themselves were in a pitiable state, and all but two of them were empty.

There was no livestock, and the cottages in the village would have fallen down if the inhabitants themselves had not somehow contrived to keep some sort of roof over their heads.

He described the house as being a Tudor building of great interest from an architectural point of view.

He did not add that the top floor was uninhabitable and the ceilings in a number of the State Bedrooms had fallen down.

In fact, when he had written down nearly twenty items, he knew, if he were honest, he could not say that one of them was in good preservation.

In fact, every inch of the Blakeney Estate needed money to make it even habitable.

"That concludes the list of my possessions," the Earl finished, "and you are, of course, at liberty to inspect and verify everything I have mentioned."

There was silence for a moment. Then one of the tradesmen rose and asked:

"Wot's Your Lordship got in London? Where d'yer stay when ye're up there spendin' yer money like water?"

He spoke rudely and suspiciously, but the Earl answered politely:

"If you are implying that I have a house or a flat, I can assure you that I do not pay for anywhere that I have slept. I have, in fact, stayed with friends."

"An' I suppose yer friends provides yer with yer food, wine, an' women!"

There was a roar of laughter at this, which Aleda felt unhappily was like the baying of hungry wolves.

"That is correct," the Earl said quickly.

As if he wished to avoid any more such remarks, he said:

"Well, let us get down to business. Is there anybody here who will make an offer for Blake Hall and the thousand acres of land that surround it?"

There was silence, and Aleda saw Lord Fulbourne and his friends look at one another.

She was quite certain that none of them would wish to possess another House when they already had ancestral mansions of their own, or would come into one on their father's death.

"Surely someone can make an offer?" the Earl questioned, breaking the silence.

Another man a little farther back in the room rose.

"If yer asks me," he said in a nasty tone of voice, "yer wastin' our time! A rubbish-'eap like this won't settle yer debts, and th' sooner we takes Yer Lordship in front of th' Magistrates, th' sooner yer can cool yer 'eels in th' Fleet!"

The way he spoke was so unpleasant that only by a tremendous effort at self-control did Aleda prevent herself from giving a cry of horror.

Her brother, however, faced the man and she was proud of him.

"What would you gain by that?" he asked in a slow, drawling voice. "What my sister has suggested, and I have agreed, is that we should both find work of some sort, then anything we earn will be given to the person you choose, to give those who are owed the most."

Two or three men sprang to their feet.

"Work?" one of them shouted. "Wot d'yer think th' likes o' yer could do—sweep a crossing?"

Other men were also jeering and making lewd suggestions which, fortunately, because their words tumbled over each other, Aleda did not understand.

Lord Fulbourne looked at the gentlemen next to him, and they were wondering if they should intervene.

Then, as further insults were being flung about the room, Lord Fulbourne rose and said:

"Surely, Blakeney, there is something in the house you could sell?"

Aleda was aware that he was implying that he would buy anything within reason.

Then, above the noise the men were making, another man's voice rang out:

"Show us somethin' worth fifteen thousand pounds, which be wot yer owes us!"

Aleda clasped her hands together until the knuckles went white.

Then every man in the hall seemed to be shouting abuse at the Earl.

It was impossible to distinguish one word from another, except to know that they became more and more offensive.

The Earl could only stand looking at them, and now there was a sarcastic smile on his lips as if he despised them for the way they were behaving.

Then from the back of the Hall a man walked slowly to where the Earl was standing.

Even when he was right beside him, the Earl was

31

not aware of his presence; it was Lord Fulbourne who saw him first and said to the man beside him:

"That is Winton! What is he doing here?"

Aleda also looked at him in surprise.

He had not shaken hands with her or David, and she thought he must have arrived late so that they had not noticed him come into the Banqueting Hall.

Now, as he stood beside her brother, she realised he was good-looking, broad-shouldered, and taller than David or any of his three friends.

He stood for a moment just looking at the screeching crowd.

Then he held up his hand and, because there was an air of authority about him, surprisingly the voices died away and there was silence.

"I have something to suggest, Gentlemen," he said in a deep voice which seemed for the moment to have a mesmerizing quality about it, "and I want you to listen to me.

"I have a proposition to put to His Lordship which I believe will be to his advantage and yours. But because he has no idea what it is, I would wish to speak to him alone."

He paused before he continued:

"I therefore suggest that while we are away talking, you avail yourselves of the refreshments I have brought with me in my carriage. My groom has orders to give them to anybody who asks, with a glass of wine."

As he spoke, he drew a gold watch from his waistcoat pocket, glanced down at it, and said:

"I suggest you avail yourselves of my hospitality for the next quarter-of-an-hour, then return here to learn whether or not my suggestion to the Earl of Blakeney has been accepted."

As he finished speaking, he turned to Aleda, saying:

"Perhaps Your Ladyship would lead the way to where I can talk to both you and your brother?"

Aleda rose to her feet.

She was aware as she did so that everybody in the Banqueting Hall was beginning to chatter to one another in a very different tone from that they had previously used.

Without speaking she rose and hurried to the door so that they could leave first, and was aware as she did so that she was followed by the stranger and her brother.

She walked ahead of them into the hall.

She thought perhaps when the traders now went outside to get the drinks they had been promised, some of those who were curious might look into the Drawing-Room.

She therefore went on down the passage to the Library.

It was a large and at one time very beautiful room. But just like everywhere else in the house, the long, diamond-paned windows were cracked or broken.

The velvet curtains were faded, and the lining was in shreds.

All the good furniture had been sold.

The books, too, which covered the shelves, had been sorted through for anything that was worth selling.

They had fetched very little, and although Aleda had prayed there might be a first folio of Shakespeare or an early printing of Chaucer amongst them, she had been disappointed.

There were, however, two armchairs, the leather of which was torn, a fire-stool that had a leg broken and a tapestry cover that was in shreds.

She led the way into the room, wondering frantically as she did so what this newcomer would suggest.

Although he was good-looking, she thought his clothes were not nearly as smart as David's, in which case he was not likely to be rich.

His cravat, however, was well-tied, but as she glanced down at his boots, she was aware they were not the fashionable Hessians.

She thought they were well-worn, and was sure, therefore, their wearer could not afford better.

"He is just raising our hopes," she told herself.

She felt angry because she knew her brother was optimistically hoping he had been saved at the last minute.

Because she knew it was expected, she seated herself in one of the armchairs.

The stranger indicated with a gesture of his hand that David should take the other.

Then he stood in front of the fireplace which was still filled with the ashes of a log fire that had burnt there in the winter.

He looked first at the Earl, then at Aleda.

She thought there was a faint twinkle in his eye as he looked at the feathers and flowers in her bonnet, and she considered it impertinent.

"I think first," he said after a long silence, "that I should introduce myself. My name is Doran Winton."

Aleda glanced at her brother's face and saw no sign of recognition in it. Mr. Winton continued:

"I came here today because I happened to be in the Morning-Room at Whites Club when you announced that this meeting was to take place."

"You are a member of Whites?" the Earl asked in surprise. "I have never seen you there!"

"I have only recently returned from abroad," Mr. Winton replied, "and I am, although you may think it strange, extremely sympathetic."

The Earl did not reply, but looked resentful, as if he disliked sympathy from a stranger.

"I have therefore," Mr. Winton went on, "thought of a solution to your problem."

"The only possible solution," the Earl said, "is that somebody should buy the house and the estate from me."

Aleda felt a sinking feeling in her heart as her brother spoke.

She was sure that Mr. Winton had no intention of doing so, and that his intervention was only prolonging the agony.

"I have not yet had a chance of discussing your position," Mr. Winton said as if the Earl had not spoken, "but I heard one of your creditors mention a sum of fifteen thousand pounds."

"I should think that is about right," the Earl answered.

He spoke as if the words were dragged from him.

Aleda knew that he thought this conversation was a waste of time and that Winton, whoever he was, was just making a nuisance of himself.

"Fifteen thousand pounds!" Mr. Winton repeated reflectively. "And yet I imagine if it were in good order and the house restored, it would be worth much more than that!"

"Of course it would!" the Earl said angrily. "But you can see for yourself what has happened in the years I was away in France with Wellington's Army. And while my father struggled to keep his head above water, he found it impossible to do so."

His voice had sharpened as he spoke, and now he put his hands on the arms of the chair as if to rise as he went on:

"What is the point of wasting time? If they want to take me before the Magistrates—let them do so!"

Aleda gave a little cry, and Mr. Winton said quietly:

"Sit down!"

It was a command, and almost as if his Commander-in-Chief had spoken, the Earl did as he was told.

"Now listen to me," Mr. Winton said, "and this is not a moment for heroics!"

The Earl stiffened, but he did not get up as Mr. Winton went on:

"I will pay your creditors what they are due and I will take over your house and estate. I have some work for you to do which I think you would find extremely interesting and at the same time lucrative. I will also marry your sister!"

For a moment both the Earl and Aleda stared at him almost open-mouthed.

Then, in a voice that did not sound like his own, the Earl asked:

"Are you—serious?"

"Completely!" Mr. Winton replied. "I admit it is unusual, but that is my proposition, and it is something over which I do not intend to argue. Your answer is either 'Yes,' or 'No'!"

"But we do not—know anything about—you," the Earl said hesitatingly.

"I assure you my credentials are in order, and the Bank of England will honour my cheques."

The Earl put his hand up to his forehead.

"I can hardly believe what you have just said to me is true!"

"I think I have made it perfectly clear," Mr. Winton said.

"Do you really mean . . . ?" the Earl began.

Now there was a light in his eyes that had not been there before.

It was then that Aleda rose from the chair in which she had been sitting.

"I can only thank you for your generosity to my brother, but of course you will . . . understand that it is quite . . . impossible for me to . . . marry you!"

Mr. Winton turned to look at her, and it was the first time he had done so since he had begun to speak.

She had the strange feeling that he was appraising her, at the same time not entirely physically.

It was if he were looking into the depths of her in a way that somehow made her afraid.

Then as she lifted her chin defiantly he said:

"Is that your final word, Lady Aleda?"

"Of course it is!" she answered. "You can hardly expect me to accept anything so utterly ridiculous!"

As she spoke, her eyes met his.

She was aware that they were the steely grey that somehow made her think of frost, and the cold winds of March.

Then as she lifted her chin still higher he turned and walked towards the door.

He had reached it before the Earl asked:

"Where are you going?"

"I am leaving," Mr. Winton said. "My proposition has been refused, and there is no longer any reason for me to stay."

"But you cannot go!" the Earl cried frantically.

"I am sorry," Mr. Winton replied, "but my offer has to be taken as a whole, or I withdraw it completely!"

The Earl walked towards him.

"Please," he said, "please wait while I speak to my sister."

Mr. Winton drew his watch from his waist-coat pocket and looked at it.

"You have four minutes," he said, "before those who are hounding you will return to the Banqueting Hall."

As he spoke, he turned and walked to the far end of the Library.

The bookcases which jutted out into the room hid him from view, and the Earl went to his sister's side.

"For God's sake, Aleda!" he said in a low voice. "This man could save me!"

"H-how can I marry somebody I have . . . never seen before today?" Aleda murmured.

"He has at least offered you marriage!" the Earl retorted.

They both knew he was referring to Sir Mortimer Shuttle, and Aleda shuddered.

"But . . . if I marry him I will . . . become his . . . wife!"

"The alternative is to starve here while I am behind bars!" the Earl remarked.

Aleda drew in her breath.

There was no doubt that was what David's creditors intended, and she knew she could not sacrifice anyone she loved to what would be a living hell.

At the same time—marriage—to a man she had never seen or spoken to until this moment!

How could she contemplate anything so horrible, so unnatural, so against everything in which she believed?

David's hand was on her arm, and he said in a voice that was not only pleading, but she knew was fearful:

"Please, Aleda, help me! How can I go to prison with no hope of ever coming out?"

It was the cry of a small boy, and David was no longer the dashing Earl of Blakeney.

He was the child who had told her once long ago that there were ghosts in the Long Gallery.

They had trembled together when their Nanny had been late in lighting the candles because they thought they could see and hear apparitions from another world.

She was remembering, too, how David had broken his leg out hunting.

He had cried when the Doctor set it, but had hidden his face against her shoulder so that no one should see his tears.

How could she fail him now?

How could she do anything but agree to this monstrous, outrageous idea from a complete stranger?

Mr. Winton was coming back from the end of the

Library with forceful footsteps on the wooden floor, for the rugs had been sold.

David was looking at Aleda, and she knew that he was praying without words that she would save him, and there was nothing else she could do.

"I . . . agree!" she said.

Her lips felt almost too stiff to let the words pass through them.

David straightened his shoulders, and as Mr. Winton came back to them, he said:

"My sister and I, Sir, have agreed to accept your proposition, and, of course, we are very grateful to you for making it."

"Very well," Mr. Winton said. "I suggest that you and I return to the Banqueting Hall. There is no need for your sister to be present while we come to an arrangement with the somewhat unpleasant gentlemen who wish to prosecute you."

"I am sure that would be best," the Earl agreed.

He looked at Aleda.

"You wait here," he said, "and we will come back as soon as everyone has gone."

They went from the Library, shutting the door behind them.

Aleda sank down in a chair as if her legs would no longer support her.

Could she be dreaming? Was it possible that she had just agreed to the most outrageous proposal of marriage that any woman could receive?

She untied the ribbons of her bonnet and pulled it off to fling down on the floor.

Then she put her head back against the back of the chair and tried to think.

How was it possible that this extraordinary man

should not only want to buy the house and the estate which could be nothing but a liability, but also to marry her?

She tried to think of one reason why he should do so.

Then it struck her that the only possible one was that, having come to England, as he had said, from abroad, and presumably having few friends, he wished to enter the Social World.

He might have money, but that would not open the doors of the great hostesses to him.

Nor would he be likely to come in contact with the Prince Regent.

Everything was slipping slowly into place in her mind as she thought that, if he were a "Social Climber," he would have reasoned it all out like a mathematical problem.

He would have realised that what he needed was a house of which he could be proud, and a wife who had the social qualifications he did not possess himself.

She was Lady Aleda Blake. If she could have afforded to go to London, she could have had the Season her mother had always wanted for her.

She would have been invited to Balls, Receptions, and Assemblies, which was the privilege every *débutante* coveted.

"That is the explanation," Aleda said to herself.

She felt elated that she had found the solution to a difficult problem.

At the same time, she was to marry a man she did not know, a man who had chosen her cold-bloodedly, simply for her usefulness.

41

She clenched her fingers together as she told herself that she hated him.

She would hate him even more when she was forced to bear his name.

She had told David when they had talked of Sir Mortimer Shuttle, that she hated men, and because of her hatred she had intended never to marry.

Now she knew she would hate her husband and she would also despise him.

Then she heard voices in the distance and knew that the tradesmen were leaving.

They sounded cheerful but she remembered how they had shouted and screamed at David like wild animals waiting to devour their prey.

At least she had saved her brother from that and she supposed the knowledge that he was free would have to satisfy her for the rest of her life.

She wondered vaguely what Mr. Winton had in mind for David to do.

She could not imagine what work he could do that he would not find arduous, if not impossible.

"How can we have got into this mess?" she asked aloud. "How can our lives which were once so happy and secure have reached the point where we are accepting charity from a stranger?"

She thought he would extract an outrageous return for the money he was prepared to expend.

Nothing could be more humiliating, she thought, than to know that Mr. Winton was making use of her, that her marriage was to be nothing more than a business transaction.

"He is exactly the same as the tradesmen who wish to destroy David!" she told herself. "And I loathe him!"

As if her feelings made it impossible for her to sit, and she had to stand defiantly to face what was coming, she rose to her feet.

As Mr. Winton had done, she stood with her back towards the fireplace and stared at the bookshelves.

The sunshine coming through the windows filled the room with a golden haze that hid the dilapidation and made it for the moment seem like a Fairy Palace.

Then Aleda heard footsteps coming down the passage.

"I hate him!" she said aloud. "I hate him!"

Her voice seemed to ring out, and yet it was a soft and very musical sound.

Then the door opened.

chapter three

MR. WINTON and the Earl came into the Library.

Behind them was a groom carrying a tray on which there was a bottle of champagne.

Almost without realising it, Aleda noticed that the three glasses with it were odd and one was slightly cracked.

The groom put the tray down on a table and Mr. Winton said:

"I will pour it, Jed. You see to the luncheon."

"Very good, Sir."

The man went from the Library and Mr. Winton said:

"I took the precaution of bringing my own luncheon with me, and I hope, as your household is busy, that you will join me."

He sounded polite, but Aleda thought he was well aware there was nobody in the house to cook except herself, and that once again he was being charitable.

She did not speak, and her brother said:

"Thank you very much! I am afraid we would have found it difficult to entertain you."

Mr. Winton did not reply. He was busy pouring champagne into the three glasses.

He handed one to Aleda and, looking at her penetratingly in a way she disliked, he said:

"I hope you will drink to our happiness."

She thought he was being sarcastic and wanted to reply that there was little chance of her, at any rate, being anything but miserable.

Yet she knew it would be a mistake to antagonise him, so she merely inclined her head as she took the glass from him.

"Now, before we have luncheon," Mr. Winton said, "I think, Blakeney, you must be curious to know what I have in mind for you."

"I am certainly curious," the Earl admitted, "and I cannot imagine what work I can do which, as you said, would prove lucrative."

Because she was nervous, Aleda walked away from the fireplace to go to the window.

She stood looking out blindly, thinking she had stepped into a nightmare and wishing she could wake up.

"What I decided when I returned to England," Mr. Winton was saying behind her, "was that I would build up a racing stables, and from what I have observed since my return, and judging by the conversations I have had with several owners, I think the best place to buy horses is Ireland."

46

The Earl made a little murmur, but he did not interrupt as Mr. Winton continued:

"I am therefore suggesting, Blakeney, that you go to Ireland on my behalf with a man I have chosen to be the Manager of my Racing-Stable. He is very experienced, and I have heard that you are an extremely fine rider. Between you, you should be good judges of horseflesh which will win the Classics."

"Do you really mean that?" the Earl asked. "It seems to me incredible, and something I would like to do above all else."

"I thought that would be your attitude," Mr. Winton said, "and I shall not only pay you for your services, and I think you will find it a generous amount, but you and my manager can spend any amount you like on horses which you both believe are worth it."

Aleda heard her brother draw in his breath.

She knew that what he had heard would not only thrill him, but at the same time, she knew it would take him away from London.

In Ireland he would not drink so much and spend money he did not possess as he did with his raffish friends.

"Then that is settled," Mr. Winton said, "and you leave at the end of the week."

"At the end of the week?" the Earl repeated.

Then as if he realised that he had nothing to keep him in England, he said:

"That will be all right as far as I am concerned, but what about my sister?"

"I have not forgotten her," Mr. Winton replied, "and as I am sure you will wish to give her away, we will be married the day after tomorrow, which is Thursday, from the house I have rented in London."

Aleda stifled a cry of horror.

She wanted to say it was impossible, that she could not possibly be married in such a hurry.

Then she asked herself what was she waiting for.

The house they were now in would belong to Mr. Winton, and if he wished her to leave, she had nowhere to go.

As she thought about it, she was glad he had not decided they should be married in the village Church in which she had been Christened.

She felt she could not bear all the people who had known her since she was a child being aware that she was marrying the man who had bought the estate.

They would be thinking that she had sold herself to the highest bidder!

She was aware that David and Mr. Winton were waiting for her to agree to what had been suggested.

As she thought wildly what she could say, the door opened and the groom who had bought in the champagne announced:

"Luncheon's ready, Sir!"

"I think we should eat as early as possible," Mr. Winton said to David, "as I have two things to do before I return to London."

"What is that?" the Earl asked.

"I want your sister to take me round the house, and after that I suggest you show me a little of the estate. Perhaps I could meet some of the farmers and the cottagers in the village."

"Yes, of course," the Earl agreed.

"Then let us go into luncheon."

He looked towards Aleda as he spoke and, as if he compelled her to do so, she walked towards the door and they followed her.

Although she was stunned by what Winton had planned and was also frightened and angry, Aleda had to admit that the luncheon was delicious.

She had eaten only a slice of toast and honey for breakfast, and very little rabbit for dinner the night before.

She found, therefore, when they sat down in the Breakfast-Room, where the luncheon had been laid out, that she was, in fact, ravenously hungry.

She knew David was too, and it was an effort for both of them not to gobble the delicious pâté they were served with first.

This was followed by a salmon which had been caught the day before, and after that there was a chicken in aspic stuffed with oysters.

If only Mr. Winton had not been there, Aleda thought, she and David would have been not only enjoying the dishes, but laughing because it was like having a meal with the Gods on Olympus.

At first, because he realised how hungry they were, Mr. Winton said very little.

But once the first pangs of hunger had been assuaged, he began to talk about the house.

He extracted very skilfully, Aleda thought, its history, first from David, then from herself.

"The Blakes have been Statesmen and Generals all down the centuries," the Earl said. "As I expect you already know, they figure in a dozen history books which you will find on a shelf in the Library."

"I prefer to listen to what you tell me," Mr. Winton replied.

He spoke to David, but he was, in fact, looking at Aleda, and she thought scornfully that he was thinking how much the Blake family tree would support him in his desire to shine in the Social World.

"I suppose," she told herself caustically, "that we should give him some return for his money."

She therefore deliberately spoke of the importance of their ancestors at the Courts of Queen Elizabeth and Charles II.

She related how they had been leading Statesmen in the reign of Queen Anne and was quite voluble about the General whom the Duke of Marlborough had praised a dozen times in his despatches.

Only when she paused from eulogising over their success and importance she had a suspicion that Mr. Winton's eyes were twinkling.

It was as if he were quite aware why she was being so informative.

"I hate him!" she said to herself.

She longed to get up from the table and order him to leave the house.

'If only we could find some treasure hidden in one of the chimneys,' she thought, 'or concealed in a secret room we have not yet discovered!'

They were stories she had told herself many times recently, when she had lain awake at night.

It was impossible to sleep because she was so hungry, and also because she was so apprehensive about the future.

She was beginning to realise now that the only

treasure they were likely to find was in Mr. Winton's pocket.

The "crock of gold" at the end of the rainbow was only "Fairy Gold," which was what David had spent in London with disastrous consequences.

Then as the thoughts rushed through her mind she was aware that Mr. Winton was watching her.

She had the terrifying feeling that he knew what she was thinking.

Coffee completed their meal, and it was made from the finest fragrant coffee beans that Aleda had not been able to afford for a very long time.

"If you have finished," Mr. Winton said, "I think we should start our tour of inspection. I will tell my servants to put everything left over in your Larder, and there are also some other dishes I brought down from London which I am sure you will enjoy this evening."

Again Aleda wished to say that they could manage quite well without his help.

She knew that was untrue, and with Glover having so much to do in the stables, it was unlikely there would even be a rabbit to cook this evening.

They would be hungry unless they dined on what Mr. Winton provided.

Aloud she said:

"As you have already seen the Library and the Banqueting Hall, the only other important room on this floor is the Drawing-Room."

She opened the door and, when he had looked inside without comment, she walked on towards the staircase.

As she went up ahead of him, she was vividly conscious of him coming up behind her and felt as if his grey eyes were boring into her back.

She opened the doors of the State Bedrooms one by one.

In the first two there was a ghastly mess made by the fallen ceiling.

The plaster from it was scattered over the floor and on the four-poster beds.

In the next room she drew back the curtains for him to see a fine painting on the ceiling and carving over the doors.

There was no furniture except for the bed which no one had wished to buy because it was so large.

They then went from room to room, and these were just as empty, except that occasionally there was a chair that was broken, or a gilt-framed mirror that was cracked.

Now they came to the room in which Aleda herself slept.

She had collected everything that was not saleable and draped her bed with muslin curtains.

There was the scent of the flowers she had arranged on her dressing-table, and a chest of drawers on either side of her bed.

She saw Mr. Winton look at them.

She wondered if he understood that because they were beautiful and unspoilt, they somehow compensated her for the dust and devastation in the rest of the house.

"This is my room," she said in a cold, aloof voice, "and next door is the Master Suite which consists of the Earl's bedroom where David sleeps, also my mother's bedroom, which is just as she left it, and a *boudoir*."

She took Mr. Winton into all the rooms and

thought he must be impressed with the huge, heavily carved four-poster in the Earl's bedroom.

It was hung with red silk curtains that were faded until parts of them were also white.

But the exquisitely embroidered coat-of-arms over the bedhead seemed to be as bright as it had been when it had first been worked.

The rugs, however, had gone from the floor, which needed polishing.

The furniture which David used was a chest-of-drawers taken from one of the Servants' Rooms and chairs which it was thought had woodworm in them, and had therefore been unsaleable.

There was a picture over the mantelpiece of their grandfather in his Peer's robes.

It was badly in need of cleaning and the frame was damaged.

As Aleda looked up at him, she thought he was looking superciliously down his aristocratic nose.

He obviously despised this "upstart" who was presuming to take over the family house in order to glorify his own importance.

"You are right, Grandpapa," she said in her heart. "He is an outsider."

She felt he understood, and it gave her a new courage and fortified her pride.

She then went out of the room, saying to Mr. Winton as she did so:

"On the second floor are the secondary guest-rooms. They are mostly empty, at least there is nothing left we could sell—and the third floor is completely uninhabitable."

Mr. Winton made no reply, but he did not ask to see any more and they went down the stairs to where the Earl was waiting for them in the Hall.

"I have ordered two horses," he said to Mr. Winton, "one which brought me down from London yesterday. I thought you would prefer to ride one of your own."

"Thank you, that is what I would wish," Mr. Winton said.

He turned to Aleda.

"Thank you for showing me round the house, Miss Blake," he said, "no—I think in the circumstances it would be proper for me to address you as 'Aleda.'"

She made no comment, and he added:

"In case you have forgotten, my name is Doran."

Again Aleda did not speak and he walked towards the front door followed by the Earl.

Without asking why she should do so, Aleda went to the top of the steps to watch them ride away.

Then, she knew that her reason for doing so was to see how Mr. Winton rode.

As the two men trotted their horses down towards the bridge that spanned the stream, and let them into the Park, she had to admit that he rode as well as David.

She had wanted to find fault, but it was impossible.

Her father had been an outstanding rider and Aleda had been put on a horse's back almost before she could walk.

She knew that a man should ride as if he were part of the horse.

She hated Mr. Winton and would have liked to be able to say that he was ham-fisted and heavy in the saddle.

But she knew, as she watched him ride through the Park under the oak trees, that in fact he was, with the exception of her father and her brother, one of the best riders she had ever seen.

"I suppose," she said as she went back into the house, "this means we shall have one interest in common."

Then as she thought of him as her husband, she felt herself shiver.

She went into the Breakfast Room and found that the cups, plates, and dishes they had used at luncheon were being cleared away by Mr. Winton's servants.

As she had no wish to talk to them, she quickly left the room and went into the Banqueting Hall.

It was just as the tradesmen had left it, with the chairs pushed about in disarray, and the floor covered with pieces of paper and other rubbish.

'At least I shall not have to tidy this up,' Aleda thought.

She walked into the Drawing-Room, and because it was so closely connected with her mother, she wondered what she would think of what had happened today.

She supposed Mr. Winton intended to restore the house to its former glory.

She had no idea what his taste would be, or if it would ever look as it had done when she was a child and she had believed it to be a Fairy Palace.

If she shut her eyes she could still see the pictures that had hung on the walls, and the mirrors reflecting the crystal chandeliers.

The Aubusson carpet, which had covered the floor

and the rose-garden outside, had made brilliant patches of colour.

It was only when her father had not enough money that he began to sell some of the treasures which had accumulated down the centuries.

It was then Aleda had been aware that things were difficult and that he was very worried.

The War made everything worse, and when David was in France, her father had died.

She suddenly found herself with nothing with which to pay the servants, and no money with which to buy food.

Now she had lost her home, and everything that was familiar. They belonged to the man who was to be her husband.

"I do not believe it . . . it cannot be . . . true!" she said frantically beneath her breath.

At that moment the door opened and she heard somebody come into the room.

She had been so deep in her thoughts that it took her a moment to compose herself.

She supposed it was Mr. Winton, and knew she must turn round and make herself pleasant.

She could hear him walking towards her, until just before he reached her, she turned, only to stiffen into immobility.

It was not Mr. Winton, as she had anticipated, but Sir Mortimer Shuttle.

He was looking, she thought, more unattractive than usual.

Over forty, his hair was greying at the temples and his face was red and slightly debauched.

He was dressed in the very latest fashion, but he did not look smart.

His tight champagne-coloured trousers merely accentuated his protruding stomach. His neck was too thick for his high cravat and the points of his collar went above his chin.

"Good afternoon, my beautiful Aleda!" he said in the thick "plummy" voice which she disliked. "How can I be so fortunate as to find you here alone?"

"I am expecting my brother to return at any moment, Sir Mortimer."

"Then I hope he will take longer than you expect," Sir Mortimer replied, "for I wish to talk to you."

"There is really nothing to discuss," Aleda said coldly, "as I told you last time you called."

"You were very unkind to me," Sir Mortimer complained, "and, hearing of your brother's unhappy circumstances, I have, of course, called to offer him my sympathy."

As he spoke, Aleda was well aware why he had not come, as Lord Fulbourne and David's other friends had, to the Sale.

He had arrived when it was too late to buy anything, and he hoped that the catastrophe would make her change her mind about him.

It was typical, she thought, of the way he was determined to force her into agreeing that she should accept his protection.

She supposed he had anticipated that David had been taken by the tradesmen before the Magistrates or guessed that he would have to face them tomorrow or the next day.

She might have been so desperate that she

would have even stopped to ask Sir Mortimer for help.

It was what he was banking on, and she knew he had timed his arrival for what he thought would be the exact moment when she was at her weakest.

Sir Mortimer was looking at her with a "swimming" expression in his bloodshot eyes that repulsed her.

As if he were curious to know exactly what had happened, he said:

"You say your brother has left but is joining you shortly? So he is still here?"

"Yes, he is still here," Aleda replied.

There was silence.

Then Sir Mortimer asked:

"I understood that his creditors called on him this morning."

"Yes, they did."

Again there was silence until Sir Mortimer said:

"I am extremely sorry that he should be in such an uncomfortable position, but I am sure it will take a load off his shoulders to know that I will look after you."

Aleda laughed.

"Do I really have to listen to the same argument we have had so often before?" she asked. "Let me make it quite clear, Sir Mortimer. I do not require your help, and even if I were drowning I would not allow you to save me!"

Sir Mortimer came nearer to her.

"Now, do not be ridiculous, my dear," he said. "You cannot stay on here without servants, without food, and without any hope for the future."

Aleda would have spoken, but he went on before she could do so:

"You know I have offered you anything in the world you could wish for, and I have, as it happens, already found the perfect little house for you in Chelsea, where you will be very happy."

Aleda made a little sound that was one of disgust, but he did not understand and continued:

"You shall have two servants to look after you, a carriage besides other horses you can ride in Rotten Row where I know that, looking as you do, you will be a sensation."

"I have heard all this before," Aleda said, "so, please, Sir Mortimer, go away, and stop insulting me!"

"You know it is not an insult," Sir Mortimer said angrily, "and I am prepared to swear that if my wife died, I would marry you."

"From all I have heard," Aleda said mockingly, "Lady Shuttle is in excellent health, and so are your children."

"Dammit!" Sir Mortimer swore, coming nearer to her. "You would try the patience of a Saint! I want you, Aleda, and how can you prefer starving to death in this rabbit-warren to having every comfort I can give you?"

"Unfortunately, 'every comfort' includes you!" Aleda said.

As soon as she spoke she knew she had made a mistake and gone too far.

Because she disliked him and because she considered he had insulted her with his offer of protection, she had deliberately defied him.

She should, instead, have run away to hide herself somewhere in the house where he could not find her.

He was a large man, and before she could move, he put his arms around her and held her captive.

"I love you!" he said. "And I will make you love me, then we will have no more of this nonsense. You are mine, Aleda, mine, as I have always meant you to be, from the first moment I saw you!"

His arms drew her close against his chest, and she started to fight him.

She was aware as she did so that it was like battling against steel bars, and that every effort she made, because she was weak and rather frail, was ineffective.

He was drawing her closer and closer, and his lips were seeking hers.

Then, as she turned her head from side to side, she felt completely helpless.

Now his lips were on her cheek, and she could feel them, hot and hungry, and as if they were devouring her as an animal might have done.

It was then she screamed.

She thought as she did so that Sir Mortimer was past caring, only inflamed by his passion to the point where he had lost control of every decent feeling.

His mouth was moving across her cheek towards hers and she screamed again.

The door opened.

Because for the moment he was blind and deaf to everything except his own desire, Sir Mortimer was not aware that Mr. Winton and the Earl had come into the room.

They both stood for a moment, staring in astonishment at what was taking place.

"What the devil do you think you are doing?" the Earl exclaimed.

As he spoke, Mr. Winton moved forward and Sir Mortimer saw him.

His arms slackened, and Aleda managed to fight herself free.

She ran across the room, meaning to throw herself against David for protection.

But Mr. Winton was in front of him, and because she was too frightened to see where she was going, she bumped against him and instinctively clung to him.

He could feel her whole body trembling as she cried helplessly:

"Save me . . . save me!"

The Earl reached Sir Mortimer first.

"Get out of my house!" he said furiously. "And leave my sister alone!"

"Now, look here, young man . . ." Sir Mortimer began.

"I will not listen to you, and you will do as I say, or I will throw you out!" the Earl replied angrily.

"I thought you would be in the Fleet by this time," Sir Mortimer retorted jeeringly, "or is it a question of my just waiting until your sister is utterly and completely desolate?"

Because the way he spoke infuriated the Earl even more, he clenched his fists and raised his arm as if to strike Sir Mortimer.

Mr. Winton, however, had put Aleda down on the sofa and was now on the other side of Sir Mortimer.

"Blakeney has told you to get out of his house, which happens to be mine," he said, "and for your information, Lady Aleda Blake has promised to become my wife, so if I ever find you speaking to her again, I shall call you out, and that is no idle threat!"

Sir Mortimer was so astonished at what Mr. Winton had to say that he merely stared at him while his face grew even more red than usual.

Finding his voice, and taking several seconds to make up his mind, he asked:

"Did you say that Lady Aleda is to—become—your wife?"

"You heard what I said, and also that I forbid you ever to come in contact with her!" Mr. Winton answered. "Now get out before I throw you down the steps, and hope the fall renders you unconscious!"

He spoke without raising his voice, but every word sounded like a whiplash.

It seemed as if Sir Mortimer could still hardly believe what he was hearing.

But, as Mr. Winton towered above him, he became aware that discretion was the better part of valour.

He therefore walked with what dignity he could muster towards the door.

Only as he reached it did he look to where Aleda was sitting on the sofa.

Then, seeing that both Mr. Winton and the Earl

were watching him, he went out of the room, slamming the door behind him.

David went to his sister's side.

"I should have knocked him down!" he said. "And I would have if Winton had not intervened."

Aleda wiped her eyes with her handkerchief.

"He came . . . here," she said, "only . . . because he . . . thought the tradesmen . . . would have . . . taken you away . . . and I would be . . . completely defenceless!"

"He is utterly despicable!" the Earl exclaimed.

"I can . . . only thank . . . God that you . . . came back when . . . you did," Aleda murmured. "I hate him! I hate . . . all men! They are . . . foul and . . . disgusting!"

She spoke violently, and only when she had done so did she remember that she was not speaking only to her brother, but that Mr. Winton was also listening.

Too late, she was aware that she should have controlled her feelings, at least while he was there.

Then, because she felt there was nothing she could say, and to try to explain would only make it worse, she jumped up from the sofa and ran out of the room.

She crossed the hall and tore up the stairs.

Only when she reached her bedroom did she fling herself down on the bed and hide her face in the pillow.

It was then she burst into tears.

She cried as a child might have done for her mother, for her home, for the happiness she had once known which seemed to have forsaken her for ever.

Downstairs Mr. Winton waited until he could no longer hear the sound of Aleda's footsteps running across the hall.

Then in a hard voice he asked:

"Who is that man, and why is he involved with your sister?"

"He is Sir Mortimer Shuttle," the Earl replied. "He came here by chance when his horse cast a shoe, and he called, thinking we might have a blacksmith on the premises."

"When did this happen?"

"I think it was about a month ago," the Earl answered, "and since then Aleda tells me he has repeatedly offered her his protection."

"I have never heard of anything so damned insulting!" Mr. Winton exclaimed.

"I thought the same thing," the Earl answered. "But he is a married man, so I suppose there was nothing else he could do."

"I should have let you knock him down," Mr. Winton said, "but I will take good care, as I have already said, that he does not speak to her again."

The Earl looked somewhat embarrassed as he walked across the room before he said:

"You will understand that, as Aleda has met only men like that, she is somewhat prejudiced about them."

He was thinking as he spoke that it would be utterly disastrous if Winton, knowing now what Aleda's real feelings were, cried off the whole deal.

To his relief, however, Mr. Winton said in a different tone:

"I think you must have a map of the estate somewhere. If you will find it, and point out to me the boundaries of the farms, it would be useful."

"Yes, of course," David said.

He was so relieved that Winton had not been offended by the way Aleda had spoken that he walked eagerly towards the door, saying as he did so:

"The maps are kept in what used to be the Estate Office in my grandfather's day. Come and see them, and while we are doing so, I could do with a glass of your excellent champagne, if it is not finished."

"I would enjoy a glass myself," Mr. Winton replied, "before I return to London."

chapter four

As the Earl drove Aleda up to London in his Phaeton, she felt as if she were going to the guillotine.

She was, in fact, frightened, and she felt as if a dozen butterflies were fluttering in her breast.

In the morning, when she had come down to breakfast, she had said to her brother:

"What are we to do about Betsy and Glover?"

"I forgot to tell you," the Earl replied, "Winton made arrangements about them before he left."

Aleda, who had worried about it in the night, thought he might have told her before, but she asked:

"What arrangements?"

"He promised Betsy she could have the first cottage he built in the village, and has given her the wages she was owed for the last three months."

Aleda gave an exclamation of joy, and he went on:

"He has done the same with Glover and told them

in the meantime they can put anything they want in the way of food down to an account which he will pay."

Although she was hating Mr. Winton, Aleda had to admit this was generous.

At the same time, she knew she resented it because it was what David should be doing, not this man who had taken them over as if they were commodities.

It made her feel as if she were just a shadow of herself, to be ordered about in any way he required.

Then, as she thought of it, he was even more frightening than he was before.

At the same time, she was determined not to be bullied or become subservient merely because he was rich.

Somehow she thought she would teach him that it was blue blood that counted, not material assets.

When she came to pack her clothes, she thought it really was a case of King Cophetua and the Beggar Maid.

Everything she took out of the wardrobe was threadbare and almost in rags.

There was only her mother's gown that was decent, and the bonnet, over-decorated with the ostrich feathers and flowers.

She thought actually she ought to take away the decorations which she had added for the benefit of the tradesmen.

Yet she needed it as something to bolster her courage, and however fantastic it might look, they were becoming.

Finally, with one small case which contained everything that was worth saving, and a few things which had belonged to her mother, she was ready for David to take her to London.

On any other occasion, Aleda would have been thrilled to drive in comfort behind such excellent horses.

But she was saying goodbye to her past and driving into an unknown and gloomy future in which she could not predict what would happen, or what she would feel.

She only told herself over and over again that she hated the man she had to marry.

Although ostensibly she ought to be grateful because he had saved David from prison, she resented him.

David himself was irrepressibly excited at the idea of going to Ireland.

"I have already been told that the best horses are to be found there," he said, "and if you count the number of Classic Races that have been won lately by Irish-bred horses, you will know I am right."

He talked about horses all the way.

Only when they were nearing Berkeley Square, where he told Aleda that Mr. Winton had rented a house, did he say:

"Cheer up, old girl! At least, Winton is a good-looking Chap, and an excellent rider."

"I am... trying to... count my... blessings," Aleda murmured.

"Then think, when you are drinking champagne tonight, and sleeping in a comfortable bed, that I might have been lying on a dirty, damp floor with rats running over me!"

"Do not... talk about... it," Aleda exclaimed. "I cannot... bear it!"

"I could not bear it either," David said, "and quite frankly, we both of us owe Winton an enormous debt of gratitude."

Aleda knew that in a roundabout way he was trying to tell her how she must behave with her future husband.

She knew David well enough to realise that he was really afraid that something she might do would make Mr. Winton change his plans and they would both suffer for it.

"I am . . . grateful . . . David," she said in a very small voice, "it is . . . just that I . . . have no wish to . . . marry anybody."

"Now you are talking nonsense!" her brother protested. "Of course you have to marry. If Mama had been alive and Papa had not lost all his money, you would have been launched as a *débutante* and doubtless be married by now."

As if he were determined to make things seem better, he went on:

"As a married woman, you will now be asked to all the Balls and parties, and as you are so pretty, you will be a huge success, and have dozens of men at your feet."

Aleda thought that if they were like Sir Mortimer, it was the last thing she wanted.

David must have read her thoughts because he added:

"Forget Shuttle! He is a cad and an outsider! There are lots of decent men who will make love to you, and you will enjoy it."

It passed through Aleda's mind that it was hardly decent for a man to make love to another man's wife.

Then she knew it was old-fashioned to think like that.

From what David had told her, his friends in Whites not only pursued the actresses and the women they described as "Cyprians," or "Bits o' muslin," they also pursued beautiful, sophisticated married ladies.

It was a style that had been set by the Prince Regent.

It was talked about even in the village, where they whispered of his supposed marriage to Mrs. Fitzherbert, and that he was now enamoured by Lady Hertford.

Aleda had not listened at the time because it had not interested her.

Now after what David had just said, she knew she had no wish to be pursued by anyone.

Although he would laugh at her for thinking so, she thought it was degrading that one should be unfaithful to the man to whom one was married.

David drew the horses up with a flourish outside an imposing-looking house in Berkeley Square.

Aleda, however, was looking at the trees and flowers in the garden.

She was thinking that in some way it was consoling to find a little bit of the country in the center of London.

Footmen in white wigs laid out a red carpet on the steps of the house and across the pavement.

David, having handed the reins to a groom, stepped down to help Aleda to alight.

"Cheer up, old girl!" he said again.

Aleda smiled as she thought it was what she had said to him when he was facing the tradesmen.

She managed to walk slowly and with dignity up the steps and into the hall.

A grey-haired butler led them through an open door into what Aleda expected to be the Drawing-Room.

Instead, it was a Library lined with books, the windows opening on to a small walled garden at the back.

Doran Winton rose from a flat-topped desk at which he had been sitting and came towards them with a smile.

"I am delighted to see you both!" he said, "and I hope the journey was not too arduous."

"Not at all," the Earl replied, "and I wonder if one of your grooms could take the Phaeton and the horses to Lord Perceval's Mews in Hill Street?"

"Of course," Mr. Winton replied.

He gave the order to the Butler, then as Aleda sat down in an armchair he walked to the grog tray in the corner, saying as he did so:

"I feel you need some refreshment after your journey, and then I expect Aleda would like to go up-stairs."

He poured out three glasses of champagne.

Because Aleda was feeling suddenly weak, she drank a little while David talked to Mr. Winton about his arrangements for the trip to Ireland.

She did not listen, she was thinking only how wonderful it would be if the Library at the Hall could look like this room.

She was well aware, even at first glance, that many of the books were new, and she hoped she would have an opportunity to read them.

It seemed to her years since she had read a book that had just been published.

She thought that if she were to go into Society, as David anticipated, she would seem very ignorant and rather stupid.

She had not been able to afford a newspaper; in fact, they had not bought one since her father had died.

She was sometimes given newspapers and magazines by the Vicar's wife, which described the parties that were given in London besides having sketches of some of the famous Beauties.

Aleda had read them, just as she had read the volumes in the Library, because she was alone and there was no one to talk to.

Now she told herself that if she were to make any sort of conversation with her husband's friends, she would have to read a lot, and very quickly.

It was bad enough to know that she was ignorant, without being aware that those to whom she was talking thought her not only ignorant but dull.

Without her really realising it, she lifted her chin a little higher, knowing this was yet another obstacle in front of her, a fence she had to jump.

Mr. Winton came to her side.

"I expect, Aleda," he said, "you would like to go upstairs and rest before you change for dinner. We will dine early because we are being married tomorrow morning, and have a long day in front of us."

Aleda drew in her breath.

She rose from the chair and, leaving David helping himself to another glass of champagne, they walked into the hall.

As they moved up the curved staircase, Mr. Winton said:

"I have chosen for you a gown to wear this evening, and of course the one in which you will be married. I hope they will fit, but if not, my Housekeeper has engaged an experienced lady's-maid who can make any alterations which are necessary."

Aleda, who was holding on to the banisters, stopped, and Mr. Winton stopped too.

"I think," Aleda said in a low voice, "it is quite incorrect for you to pay for my clothes until we are actually married. I will therefore wear the gown I have on, both for dinner this evening and at my wedding."

She spoke quietly and not defiantly, but she hoped firmly.

Then she saw an expression in his eyes which told her that he intended to have his own way.

"I had hoped," he said, "that our wedding would be an occasion that we will both remember in the future, and I would wish my wife to look like a bride."

"A bride who is being married in very unusual circumstances," Aleda retorted.

"Nevertheless, you will be my wife, and I have chosen the gown you will wear!"

She resented the authoritative way he spoke, and looking at him with a hatred she could not suppress, she asked:

"And if I disobey your august command?"

There was a twist to Mr. Winton's lips before he replied:

"In which case, you will find I am a very experienced maid!"

For a moment Aleda could hardly believe he meant what he said.

So for a second she defied him, until despite herself, the colour rose in her cheeks.

Without saying anything more, she walked on up the stairs until she found at the top of them a Housekeeper, rustling in black silk, waiting outside a bedroom door.

"This is Mrs. Robbins," Mr. Winton said, "who will look after you, and find you anything you require."

The Housekeeper curtsied.

"I'll certainly do my best, M'Lady."

"Thank you," Aleda replied.

She walked into the bedroom without looking again at Mr. Winton.

Then, as the door shut him out, she told herself furiously that once again he had won.

He had got his way, and there was nothing she could do but obey him.

She wore at dinner the gown he had chosen for her, and childishly, because she was hating him, she refused to look at herself in the mirror.

She had no idea that in the fashionable gown which had come from the most expensive shop in Bond Street, she had a new beauty which made even David look at her admiringly.

Dinner, as might have been expected, was excellent, and although Aleda despised herself for doing so, she enjoyed every dish.

She talked very little because David, excited by the good food and wine, and the prospect of his journey to Ireland, talked without drawing breath.

When dinner was finished, Aleda left the men to their port.

Then as she walked from the Dining-Room towards the Drawing-Room, which she had now learned was on the First Floor, she felt she could bear it no longer.

Mr. Winton had made it clear that they were to be married at ten o'clock in St. George's, Hanover Square.

"As I thought that was what we would both want," he had said quietly before dinner was announced, "there will be nobody there except for my Best Man, who is an old friend, and only when we have been on our honeymoon for a week or so will the marriage be announced."

"I think that is very wise," David said. "The last thing we want is for the Press to start connecting your marriage in any way with the sale of Blake Hall."

"That is how I thought you would feel," Mr. Winton said, "and I think, too, it would be a mistake for you to go to the Club tonight."

"I am quite prepared to sit here and talk to you," David replied.

"Tomorrow, when we have left," Mr. Winton went on, "I have arranged for you to dine here with the Manager of my Racing-Stable, and as you will be leaving London almost at dawn, it would be best for you to go to bed early."

Listening, Aleda thought he had everything planned out.

She knew it was sensible, and it would be a great mistake for David to say too much to Lord Fulbourne, or his other friends who had come to the sale.

However, she thought it was still an insult that he was not allowing either her or her brother to think for themselves.

'I am not asked, I am not even allowed to have a mind of my own!' she thought furiously.

She had, however, said nothing, but now she felt she might fight back, if only to assert herself.

She therefore went to her bedroom and rang for the lady's-maid who had helped her dress.

She was a pleasant young woman who had originally come from the country, but had been in the service of a Lady of Fashion.

She had left only because the Lady had gone abroad with her husband, who was a Diplomat.

Now, as she helped Aleda out of her gown, she said:

"Your clothes have arrived, M'Lady, and I've not unpacked them, seeing as we're leaving tomorrow."

"My . . . clothes?" Aleda asked quickly.

"So many gowns, M'Lady, and the Dressmaker as brought them said there're more to come, so you'll have plenty to choose from."

She smiled before she added:

"You'll want to look your best, M'Lady, on your honeymoon!"

It was with difficulty that Aleda did not reply that she wanted nothing of the sort.

Although she had to admit it would be impossible to go away with only one gown to wear, she resented that Mr. Winton had taken matters so completely into his hands.

He had organised her as she was quite certain he

would organise the rebuilding of Blake Hall.

When she got into bed, although she was tired, she lay awake thinking of how much she resented losing her independence.

She was being ordered about and even dressed down to the last detail by a man she had never seen until two days earlier.

"How . . . could anyone . . . bear it, Papa?" she asked in the darkness.

Then she knew the answer just as if her father were speaking to her in words she could hear.

Mr. Winton had saved David, he had saved the disaster which would have cost them the family's good name, and he had saved her.

How could she have gone on starving to death?

How, if she had refused to do what he wanted, could she have condemned Betsy, Glover, and all the other people on the estate to suffer in the same way as she would have done?

'I should go down on my knees in gratitude,' she thought.

But she knew it was impossible for her to do anything of the sort.

* * *

When morning came, her breakfast was brought to her bedside, after which she had a bath scented with jasmine.

She tried not to think about Mr. Winton as her maid helped her into an exquisite wedding-gown.

It was more beautiful than any she had seen, even in the magazines.

Of white gauze, it was decorated with real lace and the lace was embroidered with pearls.

She was well aware that, as Mr. Winton had bought it in such a hurry, it had doubtless been intended for some other bride.

Aleda wondered if she would feel as miserable and unhappy as she did.

"You looks really lovely, M'Lady," the maid and Mrs. Robbins, who had just come into the room, said together.

For the first time, Aleda looked into the mirror.

She saw not only that the gown fitted her perfectly, but also the lace veil which covered her hair was the same as the lace of the gown.

Her wreath of orange-blossom was traditional, and yet it made her look very young and very lovely.

She thought, however, the face of the girl she saw in the mirror, with her pale face and huge eyes, had not the radiance a bride should have on what was supposed to be the happiest day of her life.

"We're all wishin' Your Ladyship good luck," Mrs. Robbins was saying, "an' one thing's for certain: no man could have a more beautiful bride, or Your Ladyship a more handsome bridegroom!"

The way Mrs. Robbins spoke told Aleda that she admired Mr. Winton very much, and she only wished she felt the same.

Just to think of him made hatred rise in her heart.

As she walked down the stairs to where David was waiting for her in the hall, she wished a magic carpet could spirit her away to some far horizon where he could never find her.

"You look stunning!" David said. "And what do you think—Winton says I can buy myself a whole new riding outfit, boots and everything, this afternoon, because I shall want them in Ireland."

He was obviously so excited at the idea that Aleda could not bear to say anything to dampen his spirits.

Carrying her bouquet, they drove away in the closed carriage that was to take them to St. George's.

Although she knew it was conventional for the bridegroom to meet her at the Church, she had been half-afraid, as their wedding was so unusual, that she would travel with him.

Now she slipped her hand into her brother's, saying:

"Promise you will think of me when you are in Ireland, David, and write to me?"

"Of course I will!" he said. "But I do not suppose I shall have much time."

"I must hear from you!" Aleda said urgently. "You do understand, David, I shall be lonely with a man I have only just met."

"You will be all right with Doran," David said. "After all, he could not be more generous. Think what he is doing for us."

Aleda did not speak, and after a moment he said:

"If I have to sell the Hall which, after all, is my home as well as my heritage, I would rather you were there than anybody else."

Once again Aleda thought he was like a small boy, clinging to something he cared for.

Impulsively she said:

"I will try to make Mr. Winton rebuild it so that it looks as it did when we were children, when it seemed to us perfect . . . and we were so . . . very happy."

"I think that is what Doran intends," David said, "and for Heaven's sake, do call him by his Christian name! It seems to me, Aleda, that after he has done so much for us, you are not very pleasant to him."

He looked at her as if he had never seen her before and added:

"At the same time, you look lovely and, if you ask me, Doran has got a bargain."

"I very much doubt if he thinks so," Aleda said sarcastically.

David did not answer because they had reached the Church.

As she went up the steps and through the porticoed door, her heart was beating ominously in her breast.

She wanted frantically, wildly, to run away and say she could not do it.

She could not, she would not, marry a man about whom she knew nothing, who had bought her as a "job lot" with her brother's debts.

Then, as she heard the sound of the organ, she told herself she must not be a coward.

As David walked her up the long aisle to where Doran Winton was waiting with his Best Man, she lifted her head to look at them.

She was aware that a bride should look shy beneath her veil, but she thought proudly she would face what was coming and not be humble.

The altar was massed with white lilies, and the elderly Clergyman took the Marriage Service with sincerity.

Then, as Aleda made her vow to love, honour, and obey, she felt as if the traditional words stuck in her throat.

Doran Winton, on the other hand, spoke clearly and with what once again, Aleda thought, was an authoritative manner.

In a deep voice he said slowly:

"'With this ring I thee wed, with my body I thee worship, and with all my worldly goods I thee endow.'"

Just for a moment Aleda felt almost as if he hypnotised her into believing what he was saying.

Then she told herself that he was marrying her only for her title.

They knelt for the blessing, and the Priest made the sign of the Cross over their heads.

After which Doran Winton took her down the aisle on his arm, and they were followed by David and the Best Man.

There were two carriages waiting for them.

As Aleda and Doran Winton drove away in the first, she thought it symbolic that she was alone, not only physically, but also mentally and spiritually, with a stranger.

They did not speak as the horses took them towards Berkeley Square.

Only when the trees in the square were in sight did Doran Winton say:

"You carried that off with flying colours, and looked very beautiful!"

"That is what you . . . wanted," Aleda said.

"Of course," he replied, "and I always get what I want—eventually!"

There was a little pause before the last word, and she wondered what he meant.

Then she told herself she was sure he was completely ruthless, and started to shiver.

*   *   *

The Bridal Couple were toasted by David and by Doran Winton's Best Man, who was called Jimmy Harrington.

He was good-looking, and obviously devoted to his friend.

Because David, too, was looking at the bridegroom with an expression that Aleda could describe only as "adoring," she felt left out in the cold.

It was quite obvious, she told herself bitterly, that money had bought her brother's house, his respect, and now his affection.

It was a relief when Doran Winton said to her:

"I think you should go to change. We have a long way to go, and I do not want you to be too tired."

"Where are you going?" the Earl asked.

"That is a secret," Doran Winton replied, "but I will write to you in Ireland so that you can reply, telling us of all the horses you have bought."

"You are a lucky chap," Jimmy Harrington said, "and if it were not impossible for me to get leave, I would come with you!"

"David is going on a special mission," Doran Winton intervened, "and I will not have him distracted into looking at anything other than horses!"

They all laughed at this, and Aleda left the room.

As she walked up the stairs, she thought how wonderful it would be if she could go with David.

She knew she rode as well as he did, and could imagine nothing more exciting than that they could be together, and for once in their lives have money to spend.

Then she remembered that while now she had money to spend, it would be with her husband.

*   *   *

Driving away in a travelling carriage which was smarter and more up-to-date than anything Aleda had ever seen, she waved until her brother was out of sight.

Then, as the four horses which drew them seemed to leap forward, she realised the moment had come when she no longer had anything left of her own.

She was married to the man sitting beside her, and she wondered how it was possible to be so lonely, surrounded by a luxury she had never known before.

She had been provided not only with a very elegant travelling-gown, but a coat that went with it that was exceedingly smart.

If that was not enough, there was a cape of sables lying beside her in case she felt chilly, despite the sunshine.

"I will not want that," she said to Mrs. Robbins as she had left her bedroom.

"You'll be moving very quickly, M'Lady," the Housekeeper replied, "and, after all, it's one of the Master's wedding-presents."

It was only when Aleda had been aware of the value of the cape that Mrs. Robbins held in her hand that she had taken it reluctantly.

As she was about to go downstairs, the lady's-maid said:

"Shall I take your jewel-case with me, M'Lady, or would you prefer to have it with you?"

"My . . . jewel-case?" Aleda questioned.

"They're the jewels the Master's given you as a present," the maid replied. "His valet handed them to me while you were in the Church."

"Then you keep them for me," Aleda said.

She had no wish to see what the jewels were like but, she had to admit that, although she wanted to be critical, Doran Winton drove exceedingly well.

He had an expertise which told her that he understood horseflesh as her father had, and she was well aware there had never been a team in the stables at Blake Hall as fine as those she was now behind.

If the travelling carriage was smart, so was the groom who sat in the small seat behind the hood which could be pulled up to cover them if it rained.

For the moment it was down, and Aleda thought that the groom would be able to overhear anything they said, so there was no reason for her to talk.

Then, because her husband was concentrating on his horses, she peeped at him out of the corner of her eye.

He certainly looked as if he was enjoying the drive and, although she was loath to admit it, he looked, too, very smart and, in fact, handsome.

"He is just a jumped-up nobody," she told herself, "who wants to be socially important!"

But she could not help feeling curious how he had managed to become so rich and at the same time, to have the outward appearance of a gentleman.

They drove for two hours before they stopped at a Posting Inn, and Aleda learned to her surprise that they were to change horses.

"You have another team of your own here?" she enquired.

"Of course!" Doran Winton answered. "And I have also brought our luncheon with us together with what I hope you will consider an exceptionally good wine."

They went upstairs to wash, then found their luncheon arranged in a private parlour.

As she took the glass of champagne her husband handed to her, she could not help thinking that David would enjoy all this luxury more than she did.

It was late in the afternoon when they arrived at an extremely fine-looking house that was situated, she realised, in Leicestershire.

It was not very large but was, she reckoned, about two hundred years old.

It was a very fine example of Inigo Jones's work, and as they drove up to it, Aleda asked:

"Is this another house you have rented?"

"No, I bought it," her husband replied.

"Bought it?" she exclaimed. "But why?"

She was really asking why, if he had this house, he had wanted Blake Hall.

He looked at her with a faint smile.

"Perhaps it would be better to say it is my Hunting Lodge," he said, "as I intend to hunt here in the Winter, and I am sure it is something you, too, would enjoy."

Aleda could not deny it because she had always known that the best packs of hounds were to be found in Leicestershire.

Because she had not been able to hunt since her father's death, she had missed the excitement of it, and the thrill of a long run when the scent was good.

It was not really surprising to find that the house was very luxurious.

She learnt that although Doran Winton had bought it furnished, he had made a great many changes and a large number of improvements since he had become its owner.

Her bedroom was particularly lovely with a canopied bed, and a view over the surrounding countryside.

It made her aware there were low fences to jump and a great deal of uncultivated ground on which to gallop.

"David would enjoy this," she told herself.

She rested until her bath was brought to her room.

And she allowed her maid to choose what gown she was to wear from a great number which had been unpacked and placed in the spacious wardrobe.

Only when she realised she was wearing white, as became a bride, did she wish for another colour, but it was too late to change.

Then her maid brought her a large jewel-case and opened it, saying:

"I think diamonds'd go best with that gown, M'Lady."

Incredulously, Aleda saw there was a diamond necklace, and diamond bracelets and earrings resting on the dark velvet with which the case was lined.

There was also, she saw, a string of pearls and another necklace of diamonds and turquoises which matched her eyes.

Because it all seemed too much from a man who, while he was her husband, had no affection for her, she rose from the dressing-table.

"I will not wear jewellery," she said.

She then walked from the room without listening to her maid's protests.

She went downstairs into a very attractive Drawing-Room which reminded her vaguely of the Drawing-Room at Blake Hall when her mother had been alive.

For the moment, however, she was only vividly aware that Doran Winton was waiting for her.

He was looking very smart in a frilled shirt with a high cravat, even more fashionable and higher than those worn by David.

Instead of knee-breeches he wore the drain-pipe trousers made fashionable by the Prince Regent, and he looked very tall and overpowering as she walked towards him.

She was suddenly aware, because it was fashionable, that her gown seemed almost transparent, and the tight slip beneath the gauze revealed every curve of her body.

He watched her with his grey eyes until she reached his side, then he asked:

"No jewellery? I hoped it would please you."

"I am overwhelmed by your generosity," Aleda said.

She could not help her voice sounding a little sharp.

He did not speak, and she wondered if he realised that she was aware he was checking her out so that he could impress the Social World.

After a moment he said quietly:

"Perhaps you are right. You are very young, Aleda, unspoiled, untouched, and innocent, and jewels might spoil rather than enhance the picture."

She looked at him in surprise, then as she knew what he was implying, she turned away with a sudden sense of terror.

Tomorrow, if she understood what he was saying, she would no longer be pure, untouched, and innocent.

It made her want to scream and run away from him.

She was saved from making any comment because dinner was announced.

They went into an attractive Dining-Room with pillars at one end of it, and a finely sculpted marble fireplace.

There were few pictures, and Aleda wondered why until Doran Winton explained:

"I bought a great deal of the furniture in this house, which has been here since it was first built, but I allowed the owner to keep his family portraits. I thought later I might add some of my own."

He paused before he added:

"We must decide which artist will do you justice. I would like it to have been Reynolds if he were alive."

Because Aleda had been taught a great deal about pictures and artists both by her father and mother, they discussed the portrait painters of the past.

That, she thought, thankfully, was an impersonal subject and it lasted them through most of dinner.

Only when they left the Dining-Room together and because Doran Winton said he did not want any port did Aleda feel the terror she had felt before rising within her, and she wanted again to run away.

She was also aware that she was very tired.

She had not slept last night for worrying over her wedding, and she was well aware that she was not as strong as she used to be.

The reason was obviously because she had been able to eat so little.

As they reached the Drawing-Room, Doran Winton said unexpectedly:

"I think you are tired, and the best thing you can do is to go to bed."

"That is . . . something I would . . . like to . . . do," Aleda replied.

"Then go upstairs," he said.

It was almost as if he ordered her to do so, and she walked towards the staircase.

She was aware as she did so that he had turned back towards the Dining-Room as if he had forgotten to give some instructions.

When her maid had undressed her, she put on one of the diaphanous exquisitely lace-trimmed night-gowns which had been sent with her other clothes.

It was then she was acutely aware once again that it was now her wedding-night.

It was perhaps the attitude of her maid or perhaps because Doran Winton had not said good-night when she left him.

Then like a flood tide, everything she feared swept over her.

"Good-night, M'Lady, and may God bless you!" her maid said unexpectedly.

As she shut the door, Aleda knew just what she was thinking.

She flung back the sheets and got out of bed.

Now that the moment was upon her she knew she could not go through with it; she would not allow the man who was now her husband to touch her.

She thought of Sir Mortimer, and felt her whole body shudder at the idea of being kissed, or of any man laying his hands upon her.

She was not absolutely certain what happened when a man made love to a woman.

It was, of course, very intimate and sooner or later, it meant the birth of a child.

It was then she felt a revulsion that was even stronger than anything she had felt before.

How could she bring a child into the world sired by a man she hated and despised?

She had also believed that because David was so good-looking and she was pretty, it was because her father and mother had loved each other, and therefore their children had been born in love.

'I might give birth to a lunatic or a deformity,' she thought in terror.

She went across the room to the chair on which her lady's-maid had left her negligée.

She put it on and buttoned it down the front, and wished now she had not undressed.

This was something she had to fight, this was something she had to make absolutely clear to the man who was her husband.

She would do what he wanted in public, and advance him socially in any way he wished, but she would not become his wife in anything but name.

"I will not be cheating," she argued with herself, "he never pretended our arrangement was anything but a business one. He bought David's debts, and he bought me, but the only value I have for him is my title."

That was what she had to explain to him when he came to her.

That was what she had to make him see, from the

very beginning, that she would honour the arrangement, but nothing . . . nothing more.

It suddenly struck her that she could lock the door and perhaps talk to him tomorrow.

As she was turning the idea over in her mind she went to the door, then saw to her surprise there was no lock.

There was a handle which was beautifully made, as was everything else in the house, but there was no key she could turn, no bolt she could push.

It was then she knew she would just have to wait.

She walked across the room to where there was a high-backed armchair covered in the same satin as the curtains on the bed.

She would sit upright in it looking, she hoped, dignified, until Doran Winton arrived.

Then she was aware that, with her fair hair over her shoulders, it made her look very young and, she thought, somewhat abandoned.

She ran to the dressing-table and plaited her hair quickly, then pinned it at the back of her head, smoothing it back from her forehead and her ears.

She thought being so severe it made her look older and perhaps less attractive.

At any rate, she was sure it was more dignified and would perhaps make him more inclined to listen to her.

Then because she was afraid he might arrive at any moment, she went back to the chair.

She sat upright with a cushion at her back and waited, her eyes on the door, her heart beating frantically in her breast because she was so afraid.

She put her hands together and prayed that she could make him listen to her.

Somehow it was as hard to pray as it was to breathe.

She could only watch the door, waiting for it to open.

chapter five

ALEDA awoke with a start to realise she was cold.

She was also aware that the candles by her bed were guttering low and it must be very late.

Then it flashed through her mind that Doran Winton had not come.

She was still sitting in the armchair, but she had slipped down at the side of it and fallen asleep against the protruding arm.

Feeling stiff, she rose to her feet and looked at the clock on the mantelpiece.

It was four o'clock in the morning!

He had not come to her and he obviously did not intend to.

For a moment she did not ask herself why, but pulled off her negligée and crept into bed.

She fell asleep almost as soon as her head touched the pillow.

When she woke again it was because the curtains were being pulled back by her maid and the sunshine was flooding into the room.

She felt tired and wanted to go back to sleep.

Then, as the maid set a tray down at the side of her bed, she was aware it was her breakfast.

She pulled herself up against the pillows, and as the maid started to tidy the room, she asked:

"What is the time?"

"It's nearly half-after-ten, M'Lady, and I thought you'd like to be called, as luncheon's early."

"Half-past-ten?" Aleda repeated as if she could hardly believe it.

She was used to waking very early at home because there was so much for her to do in the house, and also because she usually felt so hungry.

Now she ate a delicious breakfast which was arranged on a tray with Crown Derby china, and thought how different everything was.

Only when she had finished eating did she ask the maid who was bringing in her bath:

"Why is luncheon early?"

"Because the Master thinks Your Ladyship'd like to go riding with him, and suggests you come down in your riding-habit."

Again Aleda thought everything had been planned whether she had any preferences or not.

At the same time, she knew there was nothing she would enjoy more than being able to ride.

She had an idea that afterwards she would feel stiff, not having ridden regularly for six months, which was when the horses at the Hall had been sold.

She had then had to rely on an occasional mount

from the horses David had brought down from London.

Now, she thought excitedly, she would be able to ride every day.

Then she thought:

'If my husband permits me to do so. After all, he might have other plans!'

"It is just like being at School!" she exclaimed aloud without really meaning to do so.

The maid turned round.

"Did you speak, M'Lady?"

"Only to myself," Aleda replied, and thought actually it was not surprising.

She had often spoken aloud when she was alone at the Hall because the rooms were so quiet that she thought there was something creepy about them.

Now, however much she hated it, there would be Doran Winton to talk to her and if it was as impersonal and interesting as it had been last night, it would be no hardship.

Then as she finished dressing, she found herself wondering why he had not come to her bedroom as she had expected.

Was the reason that he was being considerate because they knew so little about each other?

Or was it, and this was far more likely, that she did not attract him?

She knew he wished only to better himself and therefore there was no reason why he should consider her as anything but useful.

"Or perhaps," she added with a flash of humour, "he wants to renovate and redecorate me, as he will do to Blake Hall."

She glanced at her reflection in the mirror and realised the riding-habit he had purchased for her was certainly very attractive.

Of a deep blue material, it was not in the least flashy, but was, in fact, very smart.

The jacket fitted closely to her figure, giving her a tiny waist, and the white muslin blouse under it was exactly right for somebody as young as she was.

Her high-crowned riding hat had a gauze veil round it just one shade lighter than the hat itself.

It fell down her back very gracefully.

After the tattered old habit which was all she had to wear at home, she could not help feeling that her appearance, if nothing else, would be worthy of Doran Winton's horses.

At the same time, as she went down the stairs she felt a little shy.

This was the first day of her married life, and she was still a complete stranger to the man she had married.

He was waiting for her in the Library, she was informed by the Butler, who preceded her down the passage and opened the door.

Aleda walked in, then stopped, spellbound.

She had not expected to see so many books, or to find a room that was as impressive as the Library at the Hall, except that everything in it looked perfect, including the books themselves.

She stood staring at them in delight, wondering what she should read first.

Then she heard Doran Winton say:

"Good morning, Aleda! I hope you slept well."

She realised he was standing with his back to the

fireplace, and as it was on the left of her, she had not noticed him as she entered.

Now she saw that he was dressed in riding-clothes and was aware that he looked even larger and more masculine than he had done yesterday.

"What a wonderful Library!" she exclaimed with a lilt in her voice.

"I thought it would please you," he answered, "and although some of the books were left from when I bought the house, I have added a great many more on a great number of different subjects."

"Then I must read them quickly," Aleda said lightly, "otherwise we will have very one-sided conversations with you knowing far more than I do."

"Must it be a contest?" he enquired.

She felt it was a pertinent question, and there was a faint touch of colour in her cheeks as she looked away from him.

There was a short pause before he said:

"For the moment I think you will want to talk about horses, and especially mine. I have quite a number to show you in the stables."

"That will be exciting!" Aleda said. "And I cannot tell you how much I am longing to ride."

"I expect you will be as good a rider as your brother," he remarked.

Aleda smiled at him.

They ate a light luncheon, then the horses were brought to the front door.

As they rode off, Aleda felt for the first time since David had come home with the news that the tradesmen intended to prosecute him, that she was happy.

The horse she was riding was a spirited animal with Arab blood in him, and he was only equalled by the black stallion that Doran Winton mounted.

They set off across the flat meadowland just below the well-kept hedges, then galloped for nearly two miles before they pulled in their horses.

"That was wonderful!" Aleda gasped.

"I was quite right," Doran Winton said, "you are as good as your brother, if not better!"

Aleda laughed.

"David would not be pleased to hear you say that! But I am delighted by the compliment."

They rode on, and only when they turned for home did Aleda say:

"I am sure I am going to be very stiff tonight, but it has been worth every second of it!"

"I will give you something to put in your bath," Doran promised, "but I think you should take things easy and not do too much until you are as strong as you ought to be."

"I am strong enough to ride," Aleda said quickly.

She was afraid that he might curtail something that was an excitement and a joy, and which she had not expected on her honeymoon.

Then, as he did not reply, she added:

"I am, in fact, very strong, and I dislike people fussing over me."

"We all feel like that," Doran replied. "At the same time, one has to be sensible enough to realise it is for one's own good."

"Now you are talking like my Nanny, who always said it was 'for my own good' if I had to eat something nasty, or take some particularly unpleasant medicine."

Doran laughed, then he said:

"I will try not to do either of those things. But you must be aware that I have to look after you."

With difficulty Aleda prevented herself from saying that she could not think why.

Then she knew it was because, if nothing else, she had a certain value in his eyes.

She could give him an introduction to the privileged Society which was known as the *Beau Ton*.

She thought a little cynically it would not be difficult for him to get all he desired when he had so much money.

He could ask people to stay at his house in London, at his Hunting Lodge in Leicestershire, and, of course, when it was finished, Blake Hall.

She was sure there would not be many refusals to his invitations.

Because it was in her mind, she said:

"I suppose, when we return to London and the Season will be in full swing, you will wish to give a Ball."

"I had thought of it," Doran replied, "because I thought it was something you would enjoy, and mostly because you have never had a Season as a *débutante*."

"You are thinking . . . of me?" Aleda asked incredulously.

"Who else?" he replied. "I do not enjoy Balls myself, and find Social functions extremely boring."

Aleda was so astonished that she could not think what to reply.

Could it be true what he was saying, or was he just pretending?

She did not know the answer, and it puzzled her until they arrived back at the house.

Tea was laid in the Drawing-Room, then again with an air of authority which annoyed her, Doran sent her up to lie down.

She was glad then to take off her riding-habit and creep into bed.

However she may deny it, she knew she was not as strong as she had been two years ago, and she fell asleep almost as soon as she lay down.

* * *

When she awoke she found to her astonishment that it was night-time, and there was only one candle burning beside the bed.

She realized, because the curtains were drawn, that she must have been asleep for a long time.

With an effort she forced herself to get out of bed and look at the clock, and could hardly believe her eyes when she found it was after midnight.

It seemed incredible that she should have slept without being woken for dinner, and knew that it had been on her husband's instructions.

She got back into bed and shut her eyes.

At least she did not have to worry tonight about him coming to her room.

She wondered if he disliked dining alone or had merely been pleased to prove his point that she was not as strong as she ought to be.

* * *

The next morning, Aleda rang her bell early and was downstairs in the Breakfast-Room when Doran came in from the stables.

She guessed he had gone there to see the horses and thought it was something she too would like to do.

When he came in to find her waiting for him he said:

"Before you berate me for letting you sleep, let me say that I considered you had earned it!"

"How did you know I was going to berate you?" Aleda asked.

"I saw that accusing look in your eyes," Doran replied, "and guessed what was coming."

"Then I will just say thank you for being so considerate," she said. "I was more tired than I thought I was."

"Not too tired, I hope, to come driving with me this morning," he said.

"Driving . . . not riding?"

"We will ride this afternoon, if you feel energetic enough, but I want to show you my new estate, and the improvements I intend to make to it."

She kept telling herself when they were driving from farm to farm and through land that was being cultivated in the most up-to-date manner, that it was easy for somebody as rich as Doran.

And yet she had to acknowledge that it was more than just money.

He had new ideas and he was putting them into practice, while he was well aware that the majority of farmers were standing off their labourers because the war was over.

That meant that the price of crops had fallen.

Doran, on the other hand, had taken on more

men and found a market for what they produced and was not only felling trees, but planting them.

Because she was curious, Aleda could not help asking:

"How is it that you know so much about English farming, when you say you have been abroad for a long time?"

"I was brought up in England," he replied, "and while I have been making money from very different products, I do understand how to produce what is wanted and sell it at the right time and at the right price."

She thought somewhat scornfully that he sounded very much a tradesman.

At the same time, she knew his estate was being profitably run, which was exceptional, and undoubtedly an example to other landlords.

She thought, too, that his farmers had been very pleased to see him, and when they talked to men in the fields or in the woods, they had looked at him admiringly.

She was well aware there was the same expression on the faces of his servants.

"Money! Just money! Money! Money!" she said to herself.

Then she knew she was being unfair, and what was needed first was brains and vision.

Only after they had been riding in the afternoon, for only a short time because Doran thought she might be tired, did she have the chance of going to the Library.

She was astonished at the variety of books she found there.

As she took two of them upstairs when she went

to rest, she thought that they would open up new horizons for her.

She had to admit, however, that the discussions she had with Doran were even more interesting and enlightening.

He had sent her to bed early, and she almost resented not being able to go on talking to him.

But because he was so firm she said almost petulantly:

"You are treating me like a . . . child!"

"On the contrary," he retorted. "I am treating you like a woman, who will be even more beautiful when she is not so thin, and has a sparkle in her eyes, which regrettably is not often there."

She was so astonished at what he said that she could only stare at him.

Then because she could not think of an answer, she went upstairs to bed without saying anything more.

"Am I really so thin?" she asked herself as she looked in the mirror after she had undressed.

She studied her reflection and knew it was true.

Even the exquisite gowns she wore had not deceived him into thinking she was just slender.

She also disliked the reference to her eyes, thinking perhaps he was perceptively aware that she hated him.

Also that she actually resented that he was so rich while she and David had been so poor.

"One thing is quite certain," she told herself wryly, "I do not attract him, and that makes everything very much better than I expected it to be."

And yet, because she was a woman, she could not help thinking it was infuriating that he should find fault and not think her as pretty as she knew she was in her new clothes.

The next two days they spent riding, driving, and arguing over a thousand different subjects until Aleda realised they were duelling with words.

She took the opposite view to whatever he said.

It was fascinating to see if she could defeat him in an argument, whether it concerned politics, religion, or the strange, undeveloped parts of the world.

She was soon aware that he was doing the same, like two Barristers determined to prove each other wrong.

There was a twinkle in his eyes, which she could not help thinking was rather attractive when they challenged her.

She ate a great deal of delicious food and slept peacefully as soon as she went to bed.

On the fifth day of her honeymoon she had to be honest with herself and admit that it was enjoyable.

She had been so frightened, expecting Doran to bully her and force her unwillingly to be his wife.

Instead of which he treated her entirely impersonally. But they rode together and talked together, and it was something she had never known before and was, in fact, very exciting.

Then when her maid called her at eight o'clock she said:

"'Scuse me, M'Lady, but you'll have to hurry. The Master says you're leaving for London as soon after nine o'clock as possible."

Aleda sat up in bed.

"Leaving for London?" she asked. "But . . . why?"

"I've no idea, M'Lady," the maid replied, "but them's the Master's orders!"

Aleda could hardly believe it.

She had thought that they were staying in the Lodge for at least three weeks, perhaps more.

Yet now, after five days, they were leaving.

She asked herself why Doran had changed his mind, and could not help wondering if it was perhaps because he was bored.

She put on the gown and coat in which she had travelled to Leicestershire.

As she hurried down the stairs just before nine o'clock, she saw the travelling carriage being brought round to the front door.

Doran was in the Breakfast-Room, and as she went in he rose to say:

"Thank you for being so punctual! I can only apologise for it being such a rush!"

"But why do we have to leave?" Aleda asked. "I had no idea you were thinking of returning to London."

"I did not intend to do so," he explained, "but I have had a communication which makes it imperative for me to be there tomorrow."

Aleda waited, but he did not tell her any more.

She thought if he wanted to keep it a secret, she could not give him the satisfaction of seeming unduly curious.

She ate her breakfast.

By the time she had finished, her lady's-maid and Doran's valet were in a brake drawn by six horses, and had already gone ahead to be in London by the time they arrived.

The hood of the travelling carriage was down, and the sun was shining.

As they drove away Aleda knew that she was sorry to go.

She had been so terror-stricken when she had arrived, but everything had been quite different from what she had expected.

Now she was half-afraid that when they reached London, she would have lost what had at least been a temporary happiness.

"Why are you looking worried?" Doran asked as he drove with his usual skill along the narrow lanes which led them to the high road.

"How do you . . . know I . . . am?" Aleda asked.

She had not thought he was looking at her since they had left the house and was concentrating on his horses.

"I can actually feel what you are thinking," he answered simply.

Aleda looked at him in surprise.

"How . . . can you do . . . that?"

"It is something I have been able to do every minute since I first saw you," he said.

She looked away from him. Then after a pause she said:

"If you are reading my thoughts, it is something you must not do!"

"Why not?"

"Because it would make me very uncomfortable and after all, one's thoughts should be secret."

"Only if they are unkind or unpleasant," Doran argued.

Aleda felt guiltily that most of hers about him had

been exceedingly unpleasant, at least until the last three days.

Now she knew that she liked being with him, and after the joy of riding, she liked talking to him.

"We can do that wherever we are!" he said.

She stared at him open-mouthed.

"Now you *are* reading my thoughts," she objected, "and I shall never feel at ease with you again!"

"Then I must stop reading them," he said, "and instead you shall tell me what you think and what you want, and it is something I want as well."

Aleda was so surprised that she was silent because she could not think of anything to say.

By now they had reached the high road, and because of the speed at which they were travelling it was impossible to talk.

The journey was as well arranged as it had been after they were married, with their own food at the Posting Inns prepared by Doran's Chef.

The horses waiting for them were as well-bred and swift as those with which they had arrived at the Lodge.

They reached London in record time, soon after three o'clock.

"As soon as we arrive, go to rest," Doran said, "but dinner will be late, as I have somebody to see."

Aleda was longing to ask who it was, but thought for some reason she did not understand that he wished to leave her in ignorance.

"Why should I be . . . interested?" she asked herself as she reached her bedroom.

Yet after she had undressed and was alone, she

told herself she was interested, and it was unkind of Doran to be so secretive.

Only as she was falling asleep did she realise that her feelings for him were very different from when she had last slept in the room she was now in.

*　　*　　*

When she came down to dinner she found him already changed and waiting for her with a glass of champagne in his hand.

"Did you sleep?" he asked.

"I have no wish to admit that you were right and I was tired," she replied.

He laughed.

"Surely you have realised by this time that I am always right where you are concerned?"

"That is a very conceited remark which I am delighted to say is not true!"

"Then I will prove it to you."

"How?"

"Look in your mirror!"

She did not understand, then she glanced at the gold-framed mirror on the mantelpiece.

She saw that in some way she could not explain she did look different from the way she had the night before her wedding.

She had then looked tense and drawn from her fear and anxiety of David being prosecuted, of Doran Winton buying the house and her, and the horror of being left alone with him.

Now there was a natural colour in her cheeks, and although her eyes were still very large, her face was not so strained.

Also, although it seemed impossible so quickly, she was not as unnaturally thin as she had been.

Even her hair seemed to have a new sparkle in it, as if it had come alive after being rather lank and lifeless.

"In two months," Doran said, "you will be as beautiful as you ought to be."

"Two months!" Aleda protested. "How can you be so unkind to . . . make me . . . wait so . . . long?"

"I can think of ways of trying to accelerate the transformation," he said, "but I will tell you about them another time."

She was curious, but then dinner was served and they went into the Dining-Room.

They talked of a great many things during the meal, but still he did not tell her why he had come to London.

When she went up to bed she felt angry at the omission.

"He does not trust me with his affairs," she said, "and yet, because he can read my . . . thoughts he . . . knows too much . . . about mine!"

As she got into bed she was thinking that it was a very strange thing to think about her husband.

* * *

When morning came Aleda learnt that Doran had already left the house and regretted that he could not be back in time for luncheon.

Because she thought it was something interesting she might do, Aleda decided she would go shopping.

She was sure despite the amount of clothes he had

given her there were many things she would want to choose for herself.

There was no reason for her not to do so.

Then when she should have left the house she had become so immersed in a book in the Library that she cancelled her order for a carriage.

It was so long since she had bought any clothes that she suddenly felt shy of going to the shops.

Perhaps she would buy the wrong things out of sheer ignorance.

That would certainly make her look stupid in front of Doran.

She was sure he would point out, as he had in one of their arguments, that he had been right in choosing exactly what would suit her.

She read for some time, then because she thought she needed the fresh air and the sunshine she made one of the footmen take her across the road.

He opened the locked gate which led into the garden in the centre of the Square.

It would be used only by the residents, who all had keys.

When she got there nobody was in the garden except for two small children with their Nanny.

She walked across the grass, enjoying the sun yet feeling it was a very poor substitute for the view from the Lodge in Leicestershire.

She walked round the Square garden twice, then thought she would return.

She reached the gate to see the footman on the steps of the house waiting to cross the road with the key.

He would not do so immediately because a smart Phaeton was passing by.

There was also a child being taken for a ride on a pony and several passers-by who stared at Aleda.

Among them were two men who looked foreign and, as they stared at her, she could not help looking at them.

Then she went into the house, wanting to go back to the Library and her book.

It was nearly five o'clock before Doran returned.

As soon as she heard his footsteps in the hall she jumped up and was standing waiting for him when he came into the Library.

"You are back!" she exclaimed with a lilt in her voice.

"Forgive me for having left you alone for so long," he apologised.

"I have been quite happy," Aleda said, "and I have been reading a very interesting book, and I also went for a walk in the Square garden."

"I can see it has been one round of gaiety!" Doran said with a smile.

"And what do you think?" Aleda added. "When I was crossing the road I saw two Chinese men, and one of them actually had a pigtail! That is something I have never seen before!"

She thought Doran would be amused, but to her surprise he was frowning.

"Chinese men?" he asked. "Are you sure?"

"I have never heard of any other nation who wear pigtails," Aleda said.

"What were they doing?" he asked, and she thought his voice sounded sharp.

"Just walking down the street."

She was about to say something else when the Butler came into the room followed by a footman bearing a silver tray on which there was a teapot.

There was also a profusion of cakes and sandwiches, and Aleda looked at Doran and smiled.

"I have a suspicion that this is another way of fattening me up," she said, "and if you are not careful, I shall become too heavy for your horses!"

He laughed before he replied:

"I will risk that!"

As they had tea together she hoped he would tell her where he had been, but when he did not, she forced herself not to ask questions.

At the same time, she resented the fact that he was being so secretive.

"To make up for my negligence," Doran said, "I have invited a guest for dinner tonight. I hope you will enjoy meeting him again."

It was not difficult to guess that it was Jimmy Harrington, who had been Doran's Best Man, and Aleda found he was a very amusing guest who made both of them laugh.

They talked until after eleven o'clock, then Doran said:

"Aleda and I have had a long day and so, Jimmy, I am going to send you home."

"Are you implying I am the guest who would not leave?" Jimmy Harrington asked.

"You can stay for as long as you like," Doran replied, "but Aleda and I have both become used to country hours."

Jimmy laughed, and said he was sure they would turn into "Turnip heads."

Then, as if Doran had given him a command, he rose to his feet and made his farewells.

As the two men walked across the hall to the front door, Aleda heard Jimmy say:

"I am going to Whites before I go to bed. Is it too early to talk about your marriage?"

"I suppose as I have had to return to London," Doran replied regretfully, "I had better announce it in *The Gazette*."

"You cannot go on hiding anything so lovely as Aleda for ever," Jimmy said, "and you are a very lucky man! I know when they meet her, all your friends will think so."

Aleda felt a warmth in her heart at the way Jimmy had spoken.

Then the two men must have gone out through the front door, as she did not hear Doran's reply.

"I expect," she consoled herself somewhat cynically, "he will merely say I am improving, but have a long way to go."

She wanted to ask him what he really thought, but knew it would be embarrassing if he said something flattering just to appease her.

Because she felt somehow that the evening was not as sparkling as it had been, she walked into the hall and started to climb the stairs.

She was nearly at the top when Doran came in through the front door.

He looked up at her and she knew perceptively that he was about to say goodnight.

Then he remembered it was something he should not say in front of the servants.

It would certainly seem a strange thing for a honeymoon couple to say.

She therefore just smiled at him and was not certain if he smiled back as he stood looking at her.

Then she hurried to her room, where her maid was waiting for her.

When she was undressed and her maid had left her, she hesitated before getting into bed.

She was tired, but she was also restless although she was not quite certain why.

On an impulse she pulled back the curtains and looked out onto the trees in the Square.

The stars filled the sky and there was a half-moon throwing its light down through the leaves of the trees.

It made strange patterns on the grass beneath them.

There were also the lights from the houses all round the Square, and she thought it had a beauty all of its own.

She looked up at the stars and down at the garden, thinking that even though they were in the City, there was always something that could raise the heart in some way, just as the countryside could do.

Then as she looked down again into the road beneath her, she saw the two men she had seen earlier.

She said to herself:

"They are Chinese men! I was right! They may be wearing Western dress, but one of them has a pigtail, and I know they both have differently shaped eyes!"

She thought she must tell Doran and would run to his room to tell him to come and look.

But just as she was about to do so, the two men

turned and walked away down the Square so that she could no longer see them.

"Now I will never be able to prove to Doran that I was right," she said to herself.

With a last look at the stars she pulled the curtains and got into bed.

chapter six

WHEN Aleda's breakfast was brought to her in the morning there was a note on the tray.

She opened it and saw it was from Doran.

It was quite short. There was no salutation, and she read:

> *"Unfortunately I have to attend a Funeral today and therefore will not be able to take you as I had planned, riding in Rotten Row. As it means going to the country, I am afraid I shall not be back until late in the afternoon. It is disappointing, but I shall look forward to seeing you at dinner.*
>
> > *Doran."*

Aleda read it through twice and thought that once again she had a long day to face with nothing to do.

If she had been in the country she would have ridden, and if she had been at Blake Hall there would have been a thousand things requiring her attention.

Instead, she could only look forward to reading and perhaps once again walking in the Square garden.

Then she told herself she should not be so childish.

She was young, she had a whole stable of horses and carriages at her disposal.

Surely she could find something more interesting than just moping about in the house?

"I will go shopping!" she decided, and ordered the carriage for half-past ten.

When she was dressed in one of the attractive gowns Doran had bought for her, she thought at least she would command attention in the shops because she looked so rich.

"Money will buy anything!" she told herself cynically, and felt as if she heard a voice say quite distinctly:

"Except love!"

That was something she did not want to think about because she could not bear to go back to the dreams which were hers before she had been disillusioned by Sir Mortimer Shuttle.

Then there had been her "Prince Charming" who she had imagined would approach her tenderly and gently.

He would not insult her with proposals which were wicked and immoral, nor be like Doran, who was indifferent to everything but his own interests.

She was the bride he had bought with a house and an estate and was just part of the bargain.

Yet, whatever he was like, she wished he were with her today.

They could argue over something she had just read, or he would tell her interesting things she had never known before.

What he had never discussed was his life before he appeared like a Genie at Blake Hall.

She was curious, but she had no wish for him to snub her if she asked questions.

She thought if he wanted her to know anything about him, he would undoubtedly have spoken of it by now.

"Why is he so mysterious?" she asked herself angrily.

Then in her mind's eye she saw him riding superbly, as he had done in Leicestershire, or driving a Four-in-Hand with an expertise that she knew proclaimed him a "Corinthian" whether he acknowledged it or not.

She had no wish to go on thinking about him, so she went downstairs.

She deliberately chose several more books in the Library that she wanted to read immediately.

Even as she chose them, she knew if she was honest that they were about subjects which she wished to discuss with Doran.

When the carriage was at the door she saw that it was open so that she could enjoy the sunshine.

Only as she told the footman that she wished to go to Bond Street did she wonder if she should have brought a maid with her.

Then she told herself that while it would have

been compulsory if she was a young girl or a *débutante*, as a married woman it was quite unnecessary.

"Married, but only in name," she heard a voice jeering inside her.

Then she forced the thought away from her mind.

She knew the name of the shop from which Doran had bought the majority of her gowns, and when she got there she discovered it was kept by a Frenchwoman.

She thought vaguely she had heard her mother speak of *Madame* Bertin as being the Dressmaker to the smartest women in Society.

When she gave her name she was made welcome and *Madame* herself attend to her.

"*Voilà, je comprends,*" she said in her broken accent, "why *Monsieur* so insistent Your Ladyship's gown should be parfait! *Vous êtes très belle . . . alors, faut toujours avoir ce qu'il y a de mieux!*"

Aleda smiled at the compliment and replied:

"My husband ordered my gowns in a great hurry. I would like to see what else you have, and choose some for myself."

Madame Bertin was delighted, and when gowns and materials of every sort and description were brought for Aleda's approval, she kept saying:

"Thees ees what *Monsieur* would like! Theese, *Madame,* will make *vous ravissante pour Monsieur*!"

Aleda tried on a gown that was brilliant green, but *Madame* Bertin threw up her hands in horror.

"*Mais non, non!*" she said "Thees ees not for you! *Monsieur n'approuvera pas!* 'E would be *très fâché avec moi* for letting you buy eet!"

'Doran—always Doran!' Aleda thought to herself.

In fact, she found it difficult to choose anything that was not very much the same as he had already bought for her.

Finally in desperation she purchased a gown that was half-finished. *Madame* Bertin assured her it would be ready by the evening.

It was actually a little more sophisticated and definitely more striking than anything else she possessed.

She had the feeling that Doran would not approve.

Then she told herself severely that she refused to be so completely under his thumb that she could not even dress herself as she wished.

She went to two or three other shops, then, as if she found it irresistible, she went into a Bookshop.

She found there a book, beautifully bound, which described the historic houses of England, and amongst them was, of course, Blake Hall.

It struck her that it would be a present that Doran might appreciate.

Although she had to pay for it with his money, she hoped he would not count the cost.

It was, in fact, a very expensive book, and she had it wrapped up and took it back with her.

She thought it would in a small way mitigate the fact that so far she had always been "the taker" but never "the giver."

"Doran will understand," she told herself, "that I shall feel better if I can give him a present. Perhaps one day, although I do not know how, I shall be able to pay for it."

She drove back to the Square to eat a lonely luncheon.

Then, because she was interested in the book she had bought, she decided to read it herself.

Before she did so, however, she decided to inscribe it, and taking it to a desk, she wrote:

To Doran, his first present from Aleda.

As she left the ink to dry she wondered what he would think if she had written:

With love from Aleda.

Then she told herself it would not be true, and it was a word that had never passed between them.

It had never struck her that, because he knew so much about women's clothes, as *Madame* Bertin had implied over and over again, there must have been women in his life.

It was such a sensational thought that she found herself feeling almost shocked by it.

Then she thought she had been very stupid.

Of course an English Gentleman who was handsome, a superb rider, and very, very rich would be attractive to women.

David had explained to her extremely graphically how he had been flattered and pursued in London.

David was very young, and in the ten or more years that lay between him and Doran, the latter must, she thought, have had a great many love-affairs.

It was an idea so far removed from anything she had thought about before that she felt quite perturbed by it.

Was he indifferent to her as his wife simply because she was not as attractive as the other women in his life, or was it because he was in love with somebody else?

She had never thought of that, yet perhaps that was where he had been yesterday, and it might even be the reason he had come to London.

But if it was not a woman who was concerned, why was he being so secretive?

It would have been quite easy to say he had to leave the country because he had urgent business which he had to attend to.

She would have understood that, because he had said that he had made his fortune through trading.

If he came back to see a woman, he was obviously not telling the truth because he did not wish her to know about the person in question.

Aleda walked up and down the Library, wondering what this unknown woman looked like and if she was so exquisitely beautiful that he could never forget her.

Because she had been so much alone, Aleda's imagination was not only very active, but it gave her strange fantasies and day-dreams which seemed almost real.

She told herself a dozen stories in which Doran was intrigued, excited, and infatuated by beautiful women who were the exact opposite to herself.

They were dark or red-headed, they were witty, amusing, and very clever.

Each one of them had a sensuous, sinuous grace which made her move like a serpent.

Finally, when she was tired of thinking about Doran, she sat down in a chair near the open French window and forced herself to read the book she intended to give him.

The houses were fascinating and an artist had drawn each one skilfully.

He had certainly made Blake Hall look impressive and very beautiful.

Aleda suddenly felt a wave of homesickness sweep over her.

She not only wanted to be back in the house, but also to be there with her father and mother.

"Why did...you have to...leave me?" she asked in her heart.

Then, as she felt the tears in her eyes so that she could not see clearly, the sunshine was suddenly blotted out.

With surprise she was aware that someone had entered the room through the French windows.

For a moment she could not see who it was.

Then, as she wiped away her tears, she gave a little gasp.

The two Chinese men she had seen twice before were now inside the room, standing on either side of her.

She looked at them in astonishment, until one with the pigtail put his finger to his lips and said in a whisper:

"No—noise!"

He spoke so strangely that Aleda thought she must scream, and wondered if she did so whether the footmen in the hall would hear her.

As if the man were aware of what she was thinking, he raised his hand. He was holding a sharp knife and he pointed it at her throat.

"You—come!" he said. "Lady—come—quick!"

The point of the knife, which she knew was very sharp, was touching her skin, and she felt herself tremble.

She thought in terror that if she did make a sound he would undoubtedly stab her before anyone could hear her cry.

"Lady—come!" he said again.

Now, because she dared not defy him, Aleda rose to her feet to follow him out through the windows into the small garden.

It was filled with flowers, and a high wall made it completely private so that no one could see what was happening.

Because she had no choice, Aleda could only follow the Chinese man with the knife as he moved to the end of the garden where there was the door into the Mews.

The other Chinese man walked behind him.

Although she could not see, she fancied he too held a knife with which he could pierce her back.

They passed through the garden into the narrow passage which led to the Mews.

There was a chance, Aleda thought, that her husband's grooms would be there, and would rescue her.

There was the smell of hay and leather, and she could hear the horses moving about in their stalls.

But there was no sign of a groom until they had almost reached the end of the stable.

Then she heard voices and a man laughing.

She had a quick glimpse of three grooms watching a Chinese man showing them tricks with a pack of cards.

She was just about to open her mouth to scream

when the point of the knife touched her throat and she knew it was impossible.

The Chinese man in front of her opened the door into the Mews.

Directly outside it, so that she had to take only two or three steps in the open air, there was a closed carriage.

It was a strange-looking vehicle and very unlike anything that Doran owned.

Because she had no alternative, Aleda stepped into it.

The seat was hard and not cushioned. The Chinese man with the pigtail sat beside her and the other one sat opposite.

They drove off immediately as she thought despairingly she was being kidnapped, and Doran would never know where she had gone.

Then she told herself that, of course, if she were kidnapped, it would be for a ransom.

She could only pray that Doran would pay it quickly, and save her.

"Where . . . are you . . . taking me?" she asked.

The Chinese man opposite her obviously did not understand what she had said.

The Chinese man with the pigtail beside her, who now had his knife in the hand resting on his knee, merely once again put his finger to his lips.

Aleda was frightened, very frightened.

Yet, she thought, if they were going to stab or hurt her in some way, they would have done so by now.

She could only pray that Doran would come to her rescue, wherever she might be.

She wondered where they were going, and realised that although the windows admitted a little light, it was only at the top of them.

More than half of each window had been deliberately darkened.

Then she knew that not only was it impossible to see the people they were passing, but no one in the street would be able to observe what was inside the carriage.

They drove for a very long way, so long that she began to be afraid she was being carried out of London.

But she could see that there were still houses on each side of them, and that in a way was comforting.

Now, as the houses seemed to draw nearer and nearer to the carriage, it told her the streets were narrower.

She felt sure they were in a poorer part of London.

She was certain of this when the horse had to go slower because, she guessed, the streets were crowded, and it was difficult to proceed.

Just as she was thinking she was being taken farther and farther away from Doran, they came to a standstill.

Now one of the Chinese took what looked like a bundle of material from behind him.

As he unwrapped it, Aleda saw it was a black cloak.

The man with the pigtail said:

"Lady—wear!"

As there was no point in arguing, and as Aleda was afraid they might touch her, she put the cloak over her shoulders and tied the cord around her neck.

As she did so she realised it had a hood, and she pulled it over her hair.

It was then that the men opened the door. He stepped out and she knew she had to follow him.

She realised she was in a small, narrow, dirty street, and one glance showed her it was crowded with men of all sorts and conditions.

They were talking or shouting to one another, several were obviously drunk, and two were fighting.

The Chinese were walking on either side of her as they crossed the pavement towards an open door.

She could still see the men in the street and knew because of the clothes they were wearing that they were sea-faring.

It made her think that she must be somewhere near the Docks.

But she had little time to form an impression before she was through the open door where a Chinese man was sitting at a table, obviously taking money from those who entered.

He looked up at the man with the pigtail, who spoke to him in Chinese, then he jerked his thumb as if to show him where to go

As they walked through a curtain, the man with the pigtail went first, and Aleda again followed him with the man who could not speak English following behind them.

As they stepped into a room, Aleda became aware of a strange smell and saw the room was lit only by two cheap tapers.

At the same time, it was not empty, and she saw to her horror there were men occupying what looked like shelves on each side of it.

It was then she caught sight of a large Lascar

smoking what appeared to be a pipe, and she knew she was in a Opium Den.

She had read about them in books, and had even once discussed them with her father.

She thought then the Chinese men intended to force her to take opium, and she stopped.

She wondered if by a miracle she could run back into the road and beg the men there to assist her.

The Chinese man with the pigtail knew what she was doing and said as he had before:

"Come! Lady—come!"

The man behind her pushed something into her back, and she thought it was his knife.

She moved on to where a number of other men, Chinese, English, and an African were all smoking pipes or else lying unconscious on the shelf they had been allotted.

Then to her relief they passed out of the room and along a short corridor, and the Chinese man with the pigtail opened the door.

This room had a window which was very high up on the wall and at least it let in some light and air.

She could see that, unlike the opium den through which they had passed, the door and walls were comparatively clean and there was a bed with a folded blanket on it.

The man looked around the room, which was very small, then made a gesture to tell her to remove the cloak she was wearing.

She took it off, then, since she could not be silent any longer, said:

"Please tell me why you have brought me here."

He made a gesture which told her nothing, then, moving to the door, he said:

"Quiet! No noise!"

He pronounced the words in a strange way, but Aleda understood what he meant.

When both men had gone, the door was closed and she heard them lock it.

She sat down on the bed, thinking despairingly that if she was being kept here it would be a long time before Doran learned she had been kidnapped.

Perhaps if he did not pay the ransom they would torture her.

She was very frightened, so frightened, but she knew she dare not cry out and was sensible enough to know that even if she did, the men drugged with opium would not be able to help her.

She put her hands up to her face, then began to pray not only to God to give her courage, but to Doran because she needed him.

*　　*　　*

Doran Winton returned from the Funeral which he had attended in the country a little later than he had intended.

In fact, when he arrived back in London at nearly six o'clock, he thought that once again he would have to make apologies to Aleda.

He was wondering what she had done during the day, and decided the sooner he arranged that she had friends with her when he was away, the better.

He was, however, contemplating how quickly they could return to the country.

He thought as he drove his Phaeton through the crowded streets that the sun was too hot and the streets were airless.

He was, however, exceedingly pleased with the

132

way his team of bays had beaten all records in reaching London more quickly than he had ever done before.

But he was still late, and, as a groom hurried to take his Phaeton, he ran up the steps to give his hat and driving gloves to a footman.

"Where is Her Ladyship?" he asked the Butler.

"Her Ladyship *was* in the Library, Sir," the Butler replied, "but when I looked in a short time ago to ask if Her Ladyship needed anything, she wasn't there, nor, I understand, is she upstairs."

The way he spoke made Doran Winton look at him sharply.

"What are you saying?" he asked. "She must be somewhere in the house!"

"I'll look again, Sir. Would you like something to drink?"

"Yes, a glass of wine," Doran Winton said as he walked toward the Library.

He knew as he spoke that his throat was dry and he was wondering what Aleda could be doing.

He walked into the Library, saw the book that she had been reading lying upon a chair by the window, and went towards it.

Because the window was open, he thought with a smile that of course she had gone out into the garden and the servants had been too stupid to think of looking for her there.

He walked passed the chair with its open book, then saw there was a piece of paper lying on top of it.

He would have passed on, thinking it of no importance, then, instead of stepping out through the window, he moved back to pick it up.

When he read it, he knew exactly what had happened.

> *I tak wife. Bring back what*
> *I treasure, or she die!*

Doran Winton's lips were set in a hard line and there was an expression on his face which would have made any man, however strong, quiver before him.

He left the Library, moving so swiftly that he was almost running as he went up the stairs.

As he did so he said to a footman:

"Send Chang to me!"

The urgency in his voice made the footman hurry as quickly as he could to the Kitchen quarters.

By the time the valet, who was half-Chinese and half-Malayan, reached the bedroom, Doran Winton had taken off his smart clothes and was looking in the wardrobe.

Chang had been with him for many years and was a man who seemed to be ageless.

He had a quick brain and an intelligence which had made him on many occasions indispensable to Doran Winton.

Now he said to him sharply:

"Leung Shan has got Her Ladyship! Order a carriage and get me the Emerald Buddha we took from him."

"You give it back, Master?" Chang asked.

"That is what they want, and I should have anticipated this might happen," Doran Winton said sharply.

"You want, Master, I come with you?" Chang asked.

"Of course," Doran Winton said briefly.

Chang went from the room.

He had further names but as they were unpronounceable in England, he had always been called "Chang."

Doran was concerned with getting himself dressed, and it took him the very short time of a man who was used to emergencies and who also, as it happened, was an expert in disguise.

Ten minutes later, when he and Chang walked down the steps to where the carriage was waiting, the footmen in the hall stared at them in astonishment.

Doran Winton was wearing the clothes of a Merchant Seaman and an Officer. But his coat was well worn, and so were his boots.

Chang also was dressed like a seaman, and might have come from any number of ships in the Docks.

Doran Winton's carriage with two horses carried them to the Docks far quicker than Aleda had got there.

He knew where she would be and was aware that it was one of the rougher parts of Dockland, known as "Radcliffe Highway."

There were Taverns, cells where there was dancing, and, of course, the opium dens and bawdy houses.

Some time before they reached the Highway, Doran Winton stopped the carriage and he and Chang got out.

He ordered the coachman to wait for them, then they both walked briskly through some dirty side streets towards the Highway.

There they saw, as Aleda had seen, a large number of seamen from almost every country in the world, most of whom were drunk and looking for a fight.

As Doran pushed through them they paid no attention to him and he could hear voices speaking Spanish, Italian, German, and Chinese.

There were, of course, women enticing them into Taverns and bawdy houses, or trying to rob those who were drunk.

Avoiding the drunks and those who were out to make trouble, Doran Winton and Chang eventually reached the entrance to the opium den and walked inside.

The man behind the table without looking up at them said:

"Three-sheeling an' seexpence for pipe."

"Take me to Leung Shan!" Doran Winton said sharply.

He looked up and was about to refuse when Chang came forward and in Chinese told him what was required.

Shan rang a bell, then rising to his feet pulled aside a tattered curtain.

Doran Winton stepped through it, having to bend his head to do so.

He then went along a dim corridor with the other man ahead of him.

At the end of it there was a door which surprisingly opened into a small courtyard by the side of which there was what appeared to be a quite separate house.

Again the Chinese man led the way, and walking through a third entrance, Doran found himself in a room in which three Orientals were sitting on low cushions on the floor.

They looked up and when they saw him, two of them rose to their feet while the third, an elderly and much more impressive man, remained seated.

He looked directly at Doran Winton, and the eyes of the two men met.

"All right, Leung, you win!" Winton said. "I never expected to see you in England."

"I come, Mr. Winton," the other said, "for what belong to me."

"That is, of course, debatable," Doran Winton said, "but it was clever of you to have kidnapped my wife. You have not hurt her?"

The question was sharp, and it was impossible for Leung not to realise there was a threat behind the words.

"She safe, Mr. Winton," Leung replied. "Ees what I consseder more precious than one wife or dozen also safe?"

"I knew what you wanted," Doran Winton said, "and I have brought it with me, but first I must see my wife and make sure she is unharmed."

"I deeply humiliated Your Honour noot truss me!" Leung said.

He was speaking with mocking politeness, and there was a dangerous glint in Doran Winton's eyes as he replied:

"You have never given me any reason for doing so, and therefore you understand why I do not trust you now."

He looked at Chang, who had moved to stand with his back to the wall and was holding what appeared to be a large parcel.

At the same time, in Chang's right hand was a pistol, and he pointed it at Leung.

Just for a moment there was silence, and the two Chinese men standing to one side looked at Leung for guidance.

Quite unexpectedly he laughed.

"Alwayss trick up ssleeve, Mr. Winton!"

"And I return the compliment," Doran Winton said dryly. "Now, where is my wife?"

Leung nodded his head, and one of the others pulled aside a beaded curtain.

Doran Winton walked towards it. As he reached it he said:

"I am quite certain Chang will cope, but I should tell you that if he is not here when I come back, I too have a pistol with me!"

He did not wait for a reply, but followed the other man down the long passage.

He was praying as he went that he was not taking any unnecessary risks in doing so.

The only thing that mattered was that he should find Aleda safe.

chapter seven

ALEDA was feeling more and more frightened.

She realised that it was growing late in the evening and the sun had lost its strength.

At the same time, there was very little air coming through the window.

She felt thirsty, but nobody had come near her since she had been locked in the small room.

She sat down on the low bed, but was too tense to do anything but listen, praying that by some miracle Doran would come to save her.

In the distance she could hear voices which she thought came from the opium den, and she was aware that the sickly-sweet smell of the drug was percolating into the room.

It made her feel as if she could not breathe, and she could only pray fervently that she would be saved before it was dark.

"Save me, Doran . . . save me!" she called out in her heart.

Then she was afraid that he would not be interested in saving her, or might think it a mistake to pay the ransom that was being asked.

At the back of her mind she could remember her father saying:

"One should never pay kidnappers or black-mailers. It only encourages other criminals to emulate them."

She frightened herself with the idea that Doran would have the same principles, and would perhaps try to threaten the men with legal proceedings. But that would all take time.

She was also vividly aware that he might not know where she was.

Perhaps the Chinese man would ask him to leave the ransom money in some isolated place or force him to go alone to a secret rendezvous where they would be waiting for him.

They might take the money, then not release her.

"What . . . can I do? Oh . . . God . . . what can I . . . do?" she prayed.

She was sensible enough to know even if she screamed and beat on the wall that nobody would come to her rescue.

Certainly not the men in the opium den, and the men who had brought her here might silence her violently.

'I must . . . wait and . . . pray,' she thought despairingly.

She covered her face with her hands and thought how happy she had been riding with Doran on his magnificent horse.

She thought how fascinating it had been to argue with him every evening at dinner on subjects she had never before discussed with anybody except her father.

She realised he was very well-read, and also spoke from experience.

"Why did I not . . . ask him to tell . . . me about . . . himself?" she questioned now.

She wondered if on his way back to London he was thinking of her.

She thought it unlikely, because he would be concentrating on his horses. Then insidiously the thought came to her mind again of some beautiful woman he loved.

The idea of this other woman who did not look like her caused her to feel what was almost a physical pain in her breast.

She did not ask herself why it was there: she only knew it was, and it made her more miserable than she was already.

Then she began to remember what she had read in one of her father's books about the tortures inflicted in the past by the Chinese on their prisoners.

The terrifying "Death by a Thousand Cuts," when a man was tied up naked in a fishing net and little pieces of his flesh were hacked from him with their sharp knives, knives like the one the Chinese had held at her neck.

She also recalled that unless a ransom was paid, the Chinese would send an ear or a finger of the victim every day to the husband, father or guardian of their prisoner, until the money was handed to them.

What she was thinking was so frightening that she

141

jumped to her feet and, although she knew it was useless, tried to pull open the door.

It was firmly locked and she turned to look at the window, wondering if she could somehow reach it and climb to safety.

She stretched up her arms, but the window was several feet above them, and anyway it was too small for her to have any chance of wriggling through it.

"What . . . can I . . . do? What can . . . I do?" she asked despairingly.

Then she heard the key turn in the lock.

For a moment she was frozen into immobility, and afraid it was the Chinese man coming to torture her.

Then as the door opened Doran stood there.

For one second she could not believe it was possible.

Yet as he came into the small room and seemed to fill it, she knew it was true. He was there and her prayers were answered.

She gave a cry that seemed to echo round the walls, then flung herself against him.

"You . . . have . . . come . . . you . . . have . . . come!" she cried.

He put his arms around her, and as he pulled her almost roughly against him, his lips came down on hers.

Without even thinking, she surrendered her whole body to him.

He was there, she was safe, and he had heard her calling him.

It might have been a few seconds or a century before Doran raised his head.

"You are all right, my darling?" he asked. "They have not hurt you?"

"You . . . are here . . . I prayed . . . you would . . . save me . . . because I was s-so . . . frightened!"

"Nothing can frighten you now," he said. "Come —I will take you home."

She could hardly understand what he was saying, but her eyes, shining like stars, were looking up into his, and her lips quivered from his kiss.

Doran glanced over her head and saw the folded blanket on the bed.

He picked it up and put it round her shoulders.

Then he drew her through the door and across the corridor into the room where the Oriental men were waiting.

He felt her stiffen against him, and knew she was afraid.

He drew her in front of Leung and said:

"My wife is unhurt. Now I will return to you what you have come so far to collect."

As he spoke, Chang slipped the pistol he held in his right hand into his pocket, and undid the paper which covered the parcel.

He took out what appeared to be a beautifully in-laid wooden box.

He handed it to Doran, who took his arms from Aleda and opening the doors of the box revealed what was inside.

Aleda saw to her surprise it was a gold statue of Buddha, and she was sure it was very old.

Then, as Doran looked down at it and she knew he was deliberately showing it to her, she realised that while the Buddha was carved in gold, he was seated on what she thought at first was a large piece of jade.

Then as it sparkled she was aware that it was a huge emerald.

Doran then ceremoniously handed the Buddha to Leung.

The Chinese man kept the expressionless mask of the Oriental, but Aleda felt the way he reached out for the box was very revealing.

As he did so the three men went down first on their knees then prostrated themselves so that their foreheads touched the floor.

"As you see," Doran said, "your treasure has been safe in my keeping. In future, I suggest you follow the teachings of the Lord Buddha, so that you do not lose it again."

Leung did not appear to hear what was being said. He was merely staring at the gold Buddha as if he wanted to be quite certain the statue was there.

Then he shut his eyes and said:

"Go in peace, Mr. Winton! Battle between us over!"

"As you say," Doran replied, "there will be no more enmity."

He turned to Aleda, pulled the blanket over her head, and picked her up in his arms.

"I shall require your servants," he said to Leung with a note of authority, "to take us in safety to where my carriage is waiting."

"My men at your service," Leung replied.

Doran inclined his head, and the Chinese man bowed in the same respectful way.

Then the Chinese went ahead and the two who had stood at Leung's side followed behind, with Chang.

Aleda could feel the strength of Doran's arms.

Because she was afraid of the crowds in the street and the drunken sailors she had seen when she entered the opium den, she hid her face against his shoulder.

As they stepped out through the exit of the opium den, the noise was almost deafening.

She could not see the violent fight that was taking place between two sailors, one black and the other white.

Or a number of men who stood round them encouraging and cheering on their favourites, who were both the worse for drink.

The man led Doran quickly past them while the others surrounded him.

They prevented Doran from being solicited by the women who were attracted by his uniform, or insulted by men who were so drunk that they swayed or stumbled as they tried to speak to him.

The pick-pockets, who thought that any man of superior rank would have money they could snatch, were brushed aside.

Doran walked quickly, and it was a relief when he saw the carriage where he had left it.

When he had lifted Aleda inside, he gave the men three golden sovereigns before Chang sprang up on the box, and they drove off.

He sat down beside Aleda and put his arms around her, pulling the blanket from her head.

"This shall never happen again!" he swore.

It was then, as she felt herself close against him that tears filled her eyes, and because she could not help it, she started to cry.

"It is all right, my precious," he said soothingly,

"you are safe, and you must have known I would find you."

"I . . . I was . . . so frightened!" she sobbed. "And . . . afraid you would not . . . know where I was!"

"It is something that should never have happened," Doran said, "and when we get home I will tell you all about it, but now I just want to look at you."

He put his finger under her chin as he spoke and very gently turned her face up to his.

The tears were running down her cheeks, but he thought no woman could look more lovely, and at the same time in need of protection.

Then he was kissing her, kissing her demandingly, possessively, fiercely, because he was afraid he might have lost her.

His kiss made Aleda feel as if the Heavens had opened, and she knew although she had not realised it, this was what she wanted, and also what she had prayed for.

She felt as if his lips drew her heart from her body and made it his, and she thought perhaps she was dreaming.

And yet it was more wonderful than any dream could ever be.

He kissed her until she was no longer crying, and he felt the response of her lips and knew that she was his as he had always meant her to be.

He wiped the tears from her eyes and her cheeks, then, as if words were superfluous, he was kissing her again.

He kissed her until she had moved even closer to him, and she could feel his heart beating frantically.

She knew that this was the love which had been in her dreams.

*   *   *

The horses were moving quickly, and Aleda could hardly believe it possible when she became aware that they were drawing to a standstill outside the house in Berkeley Square.

"We are home," Doran said in a deep voice, "and I want you to go straight upstairs to bed."

For a moment it was difficult to understand what he way saying.

Then she gave a little cry and said in a whisper:

"I . . . I do not . . . want to . . . leave you!"

"You will not do that," he said, "but I want to have a bath and then we will have dinner in your room."

"Y-you will come and . . . talk to me?"

"You can be certain of that!"

A footman opened the carriage door and Doran got out first, then assisted Aleda to the ground.

He had his arm around her and she managed to walk across the pavement, and up the steps into the hall.

Only when she reached the staircase did he say in a low voice:

"Would you like me to carry you?"

"N-no . . . I am . . . all right . . . I will . . . walk."

There was, however, obviously a little doubt in her mind, and without saying any more, Doran picked her up.

He carried her up the stairs and once again she thought how strong he was, and that she never wanted to leave the comfort of his arms.

He carried her into her bedroom, where her lady's-maid was waiting, and as he put her down, he said:

"I promise you I will not be long."

She still wanted to hold on to him, but he had gone before she could do so.

Then she told herself he would come back as he had promised.

There was a bath waiting for her, and when she had dried herself she thought perhaps she should put on an evening-gown.

"You're having dinner up here, M'Lady," her maid said as if she had asked the question, "and the Master's dining with you."

Aleda's eyes shone in her pale face.

She allowed the maid to help her into one of her beautiful lace-trimmed nightgowns with a scarf trimmed with the same lace to wear over it.

She sat at the dressing-table while the lady's-maid arranged her hair before she got into bed.

It was then the footmen carried in a table and set it beside her and she saw with delight that it was laid for two people.

There was a gold candelabrum on it, and it was also decorated with white orchids.

Aleda, however, was waiting, and it was only a short time before Doran came in.

At first she thought he was formally dressed, then she realised he was wearing a long dark robe frogged across the front with braid of a slightly lighter colour.

It made him look almost as if he were wearing a military uniform.

As soon as he appeared there was a glass of

champagne for them to drink, and Aleda realised how thirsty she was.

Strangely enough, although she did not expect it, she was also hungry, and she finished the bowl of clear soup before she said:

"Now I feel better, and I want you to tell me all you have been doing."

"I want to do that later," Doran answered.

She looked at him as he spoke and everything she was going to say went from her mind, and all she could think of was that she loved him.

"I feel the same," he said gently, "so let us finish eating, then we can be alone."

*   *   *

Afterwards Aleda was to think what a strange dinner it was, when they just looked at each other and ate what was put in front of them.

Finally, the footmen lifted the table and took it away, leaving Doran sitting with a glass of brandy in his hand.

Aleda gave a little sigh and leant back against the pillows.

"Now . . . we can . . . talk," she said.

Doran rose and put his glass of brandy down on a table.

Then he sat on the side of the bed facing her before he asked gently:

"Is that what you want?"

She looked up at him and her eyes were very revealing.

"Tell me," he said coaxingly.

"I . . . I want you . . . to kiss me," she whispered.

"And that, my precious, is what I want too," he said.

She thought he would bend towards her and her lips were ready for his, but to her surprise he rose to his feet, locked the door, and walked round the bed.

He took off his robe and got in beside her. Because it was not what she expected, she gave a little gasp.

Then his arms went round her and he said:

"It is easier to kiss you like this!"

His lips took possession of her, and as they did so, she knew that her whole body seemed to vibrate to him and she wanted to be close to him and even closer.

Also, although she could not understand, she wanted to be a part of him completely.

He kissed her eyes, her little nose, then, as she lifted her lips eagerly, he kissed her neck.

It gave her strange sensations she had never known, and yet were so exciting and so wonderful that she thought she must have sought them in her dreams.

Then, as she felt his heart beating on hers and his hand touching her body, it was as if he were carrying her into the sunlit sky, where there was no fear, no evil, only him.

She knew that this was love, the love she had thought she would never find.

* * *

A long time later, it was dark outside the windows.

The curtains had not been drawn and Aleda could see the first evening stars shining over the trees in Berkeley Square.

Softly she asked:

"Do you . . . really . . . love . . . me?"

"I have loved you since the first moment I saw you," Doran replied.

"Is that . . . true?"

He could see the surprise in her eyes by the light of the candles that were shining behind the curtains of the bed.

"It is true!" he said. "But I have had to wait a very long time before I could tell you so."

She gave a little chuckle.

"Not really so very long. After all, we have not yet been married a week!"

"It seems like a million years!" he said. "But I was prepared to wait until you stopped hating men, and especially me!"

"How could . . . I have . . . been so . . . foolish?"

"It was understandable."

"I have wasted . . . so much time . . . when you might have been . . . kissing me!"

"I will make up for it," he promised.

He kissed her forehead, and she asked curiously:

"Did you really . . . love me the . . . first time you saw me in the . . . Banqueting Hall?"

"I thought no one could be so beautiful, even wearing that ridiculously over-decorated bonnet as a flag of defiance!"

"You . . . knew, that is . . . what it . . . was?"

"I knew when I saw you standing proudly in front of those tradesmen that you were everything I had sought in many parts of the world, but never found."

"Oh, darling Doran . . . how . . . romantic!"

"It was like a revelation to me," he said. "I thought you were surrounded with a celestial light and as I watched you, I knew that I could not risk losing you."

"Is that why you . . . married me in that . . . strange manner?"

"I was terrified that some other man would take you away from me!"

She knew he was thinking of David's friends who were members of Whites Club.

She cuddled a little closer as she said:

"Tell me more . . . and why you were . . . there in the . . . first place."

"I was at the Club," Doran explained, "when I heard David saying that he was to be 'dunned' by his tradesmen, and I realised how desperate he was."

"You felt . . . sorry for him?"

"Very sorry, because it is exactly what once I had felt myself, and I wanted to help him."

"That was kind of you."

"Perhaps it was something deeper than that, the Power that guides us all, leading me to you."

"Oh, Doran . . . I am . . . sure that is true . . . but go on!"

"I came to Blake Hall, not quite certain what I would do about your brother's debts, then, when I saw you, everything fell into place!"

"So you . . . bought the house . . . the estate . . . and me!"

"I would have bought the sun, the moon, and the stars if it included you!"

Aleda sighed.

"How can . . . I have been so . . . foolish as to . . . hate you? I ought to have . . . felt the . . . same."

"You had been frightened by that unpleasant man whom I will kill, if he ever comes near you again, and he prejudiced you against all men, including me!"

"Y-you know I . . . love you . . . now?"

"You will have to keep telling me so," Doran replied. "I have been so afraid that I might have to wait for years before you changed your opinion."

"I . . . think," Aleda said in a small voice, "I fell . . . in love with . . . you when I saw how well . . . you rode . . . and, of course . . . I could not help loving . . . your horses!"

"If you love them more than me, I shall sell the lot!"

She laughed and he went on:

"I warn you, I shall be a very jealous husband, and I think the best thing I can do is to take you away to the East, and let no other Englishman see you!"

Aleda put her hand up to touch his cheek.

"I would not . . . mind where we went . . . or what we did . . . as long as you . . . love me."

"You may be quite certain of that!" Doran said. "And it is going to take not one lifetime, but a dozen to tell you how much I worship and adore you!"

"When we were . . . married you made . . . your vows sound . . . very sincere."

"I *was* sincere!" he said. "And I was praying as I have never prayed in my life before that one day you would be my *real* wife."

"Which . . . I am . . . now," Aleda said.

"I did not hurt or frighten you?"

"You took . . . me into a special . . . Heaven that I never . . . knew existed . . . and I did not . . . know that . . . love could be so . . . beautiful . . . so wonderful . . . that it could . . . belong only to . . . God."

Aleda knew that Doran was moved by the way his lips touched her skin.

Then she said:

"There is so much I want to know about you, besides thinking you are the most wonderful man in the whole world!"

"You will make me conceited!" Doran protested. "At the same time, I have a great deal to tell you, and it is difficult to know where to begin."

"Then tell me first why you had to . . . come to London in such a hurry . . . when I wanted to . . . stay in the country and . . . ride your horses."

"We are going back there tomorrow," he said.

Aleda gave a little cry of delight, and he said:

"What did *you* think was the reason for our coming to London?"

There was silence.

Then as he looked at her questioningly she hid her face against his neck.

"I . . . thought," she said in a small voice he could hardly hear, "that . . . perhaps you came to . . . see someone you . . . loved."

For a moment Doran was too surprised to answer. Then he laughed.

"My darling, my sweet!" he said. "Did you really think there was any other woman in my life?"

"I . . . I was afraid . . . there might be . . . because I . . . did not . . . attract you."

He held her so close to him that it was hard to breathe.

"If you only knew the tortures I have been through night after night, wanting to kiss you, wanting to love you, and terrified of increasing your hatred so that you might run away from me!"

"Forgive . . . me."

"I will forgive you only if you promise to love me and to let me love you!"

"That is . . . what I . . . want," Aleda cried, and he did not miss the first note of passion in her voice.

Then when he would have kissed her she said:

"You still have not told me why . . . you came to . . . London!"

"The Prime Minister, Lord Liverpool, sent for me because he wanted to offer me a very special appointment."

This was something Aleda had not expected, and she looked at him in astonishment before she asked what it was.

"He suggested that I should work with the Secretary of State for Foreign Affairs, Viscount Castlereagh, and, in fact, become the Under-Secretary!"

"I can . . . hardly believe . . . it!" Aleda exclaimed. "And have you . . . accepted?"

"I have more or less committed myself," Doran replied, "but I really want to do nothing but make love to you."

"It is a . . . great honour," Aleda said, "and I . . . suppose it is because you . . . know so much about the . . . East, where you have . . . worked."

"Of course," Doran said. "But I never expected for a moment that what I had done in China would result, my precious little wife, in you being kidnapped."

"I could not . . . believe that it was happening in . . . England!" Aleda said. "And it was very . . . very . . . frightening!"

"I know it was, my darling," he answered, "but

everything is settled now, and will never happen again."

"D-did you . . . have to give him a . . . great deal of money for me?" Aleda asked nervously.

Doran smiled.

"Not money, my sweet, but something which to him is far more precious."

"You mean . . . the Buddha!"

"Yes, it is a very special one."

"Why? Was it because He was sitting on an emerald? At least, I think He was."

"That is clever of you! He is, in fact, a Gold Buddha of the Eastern Wei Dynasty, and carved in about A.D. 356. It is the most precious object that Leung possesses."

"Do you . . . mean he . . . worships it?"

"Not only he, but his whole family, and his ancestors before him."

"Then how could you have . . . taken it from . . . him?"

"I did it to teach him a lesson," Doran replied. "He tried to cheat me out of a very large sum of money. I not only prevented him from doing so, and made him pay what he owed me, but to make sure he never tried to trick me again, I took what he values more than money."

Doran spoke in a hard voice, and Aleda was certain it had, in fact, been a very fierce battle between the two.

Then he sighed.

"Leung has certainly taken his revenge. I have never in my life been so terrified, thinking they might have hurt you, as I was when I found a note they had left me in the Library."

"I thought somehow they would demand . . . a ransom," Aleda said.

"It was lying on the book you were reading."

She gave a little cry.

"That book is my present to you! I bought it today, and I thought it would please you."

"The Butler brought it upstairs to me while I was having my bath," Doran said, "and when I have time, I am going to thank you for it."

As if she knew the way he would do so, Aleda lifted her lips to his.

He did not kiss her, but said:

"I have something else to tell you."

"What is it?"

Because he spoke seriously, she was suddenly afraid it was something that would spoil their happiness.

"It is nothing frightening," Doran said, "but the Funeral I had to attend today was my uncle's."

"I wondered whose it was. Were you very upset at his death?"

"To be honest, I was glad, and thankful I need never see or hear of him again!"

There was a hard note in Doran's voice which surprised Aleda.

"Why?" she asked.

"It is a long story, but one you must hear sooner or later," he replied. "My mother and father were killed in an accident when I was twelve."

There was a note of pain in his voice which made Aleda instinctively move closer to him.

"I went to live with my father's elder brother, and from that moment on, my life was a living hell!"

"How terrible . . . but why?"

"My uncle hated and resented me because he had no son himself, and he had, I think, always been jealous of my father, who was a sportsman, while he was not, and a much admired and loved man, while he was hated!"

"And . . . he made you . . . suffer for . . . it?"

"He used every possible excuse to beat me. He tortured me mentally, and the only happy time in my life was when I was at School."

"I . . . I cannot bear to . . . think about . . . it," Aleda cried.

"Then, when I was eighteen," Doran went on, "I came to London and, like David, I found it an entrancing, exciting place, where women flattered me, and where every entertainment was possible as long as you had money."

He paused, then in a different tone of voice, said:

"You can imagine what happened. In two years I had run through the little money my father left me, and had piled up a multitude of debts."

"What did . . . you do?" Aleda asked, thinking she knew the answer.

"I was aware that my uncle was waiting for this to happen so that he could get me back into his clutches and make me subservient to him, as he had forced me to be as a child, so I ran away."

"To the East?"

"As you so rightly guess, to the East. A friend of mine was going to join his Regiment, and I went with him."

"And became . . . a trader, as you . . . told me."

"I worked very hard in a variety of ways, and had the amazing luck of being more or less adopted by an extremely astute and clever merchant."

"Tell me about it," Aleda said as Doran stopped speaking.

"It is something I want to do, but not at this particular moment. Suffice it to say that not only had I accumulated quite a lot of money of my own, but when my friend died, because he had looked on me as a son, he left me his enormous fortune."

"That was very exciting for you, but why did you come back to England?"

"I had no intention of doing so until I was informed by my uncle's Solicitors that he was dying."

"And he wanted you to forgive him for his cruelty?"

"Certainly not!" Doran said. "But his estate would come to me on his death, and also his title."

"His . . . title?" Aleda exclaimed.

"I am now the Marquis of Winteringham!"

For a moment Aleda was stunned into silence. Then she said:

"How . . . could I have known . . . how could I have . . . guessed? I thought you had . . . married me because I . . . could help you to be . . . accepted into Society."

There was a pause, then Doran laughed.

"My precious, my foolish one! How could you have thought anything so utterly and completely ridiculous?"

"I could not . . . imagine any other . . . reason for you . . . buying me . . . as you did!"

He laughed again.

"Then you have never looked in your mirror, my sweet. But it never struck me for a moment that you would think of anything so absurd."

"I suppose, as you are so . . . important," Aleda

159

said, "that is another . . . reason why the Prime Minister wanted you to be the Under-Secretary of State for Foreign Affairs."

"I prefer to think it was entirely on my own merits," Doran answered.

Because she thought she had perhaps said the wrong thing, Aleda whispered:

"I . . . I want to be with you . . . I do not want to . . . lose you because you will become so . . . important . . . and have so much to . . . do."

"You will never do that," he said, "and as a Statesman, I shall need a very helpful and, of course, a very loving wife to look after me."

"I . . . I will . . . try to be that."

Then, as if it suddenly struck her, she said:

"But . . . surely if you have . . . your uncle's house . . . which will be yours . . . you will not want Blake Hall?"

"I bought your home, my darling, because it is not only one of the most attractive houses I have ever seen, but also because I will never live or, if possible, set foot in my uncle's house."

His voice was harsh as he said:

"Even to think of it brings back the misery I suffered and the torture when I lived there, and anyway, it is an extremely ugly building which has been in my family for less than a hundred years."

"So you . . . really want . . . Blake Hall?"

"You and I are going to make it as perfect as it was when it was built, and the estate shall be a model of its kind."

As he spoke, Doran tipped Aleda's face up to his and said very softly against her lips:

"And you are going to help me, my precious one,

in living there, and also making my family name respected and loved rather than hated."

"You know I will do . . . anything you . . . ask me to do," Aleda said, "but . . . please . . . darling . . . go on loving me! I know now how . . . lonely I have been since . . . Papa died . . . and everything has been . . . such a . . . struggle without money . . . and without even . . . hope."

"All that is finished," Doran said. "We are going to create a new world for ourselves which is different from what either of us has done before."

"That . . . sounds very . . . exciting!"

"It will be exciting!" he said. "And I think together we can also create happiness for ourselves and our *children* as well as other people."

Because of the way he accentuated the world "children" Aleda blushed.

She would have hidden her face against him, but he prevented her from doing so by saying:

"I love you! God, how I love you, and now I want to thank you for the first present you have given me."

As he spoke, his lips held hers captive, and he was showering her with slow, demanding kisses.

It lasted a long time, and when Doran finally paused for breath Aleda said:

"I . . . love you . . . oh . . . Doran . . . I love you!"

She felt his hand moving over her breast and down to her hip.

Then, as a little quiver went through her, he said:

"Now I have thanked you for your first present, but, darling, I want a second one."

"What is . . . that?" she whispered.

"I want you to give me your heart."

"It is . . . yours!"

"And your soul."

"It is . . . yours . . . too!"

She could feel his heart beating as he said:

"That leaves only one more thing . . ."

She waited and he went on:

". . . your adorable, entrancing, wildly exciting body!"

"It is . . . yours! Of course . . . it is . . . yours!" Aleda replied. "Love me . . . please . . . my wonderful . . . magnificent husband . . . love me!"

As Doran carried her up into the sky, the sunshine within her turned to fire, and the light of the Divine encircled them both.

Then together they entered the Heaven which God has created especially for lovers.

ABOUT THE AUTHOR

Barbara Cartland, the world's most famous romantic novelist, who is also an historian, playwright, lecturer, political speaker and television personality, has now written over 490 books and sold nearly 500 million copies all over the world.

She has also had many historical works published and has written four autobiographies as well as the biographies of her mother and that of her brother, Ronald Cartland, who was the first Member of Parliament to be killed in the last war. This book has a preface by Sir Winston Churchill and has just been republished with an introduction by Sir Arthur Bryant.

Love at the Helm, a novel written with the help and inspiration of the late Earl Mountbatten of Burma, Great Uncle of His Royal Highness The Prince of Wales, is being sold for the Mountbatten Memorial Trust.

She has broken the world record for the last thirteen years by writing an average of twenty-three books a year. In the Guinness Book of Records she is listed as the world's top-selling author.

Miss Cartland in 1978 sang an Album of Love Songs with the Royal Philharmonic Orchestra.

In private life Barbara Cartland, who is a Dame of the Order of St. John of Jerusalem, Chairman of the St. John Council in Hertfordshire and Deputy President of the St. John Ambulance Brigade, has fought for better conditions and salaries for Midwives and Nurses.

She championed the cause for the Elderly in 1956 invoking a Government Enquiry into the "Housing Conditions of Old People."

In 1962 she had the Law of England changed so that Local Authorities had to provide camps for their own Gypsies. This has meant that since then thousands and thousands of Gypsy children have been able to go to School, which they had never been able to do in the past, as their caravans were moved every twenty-four hours by the Police.

There are now fourteen camps in Hertfordshire and Barbara Cartland has her own Romany Gypsy Camp called Barbaraville by the Gypsies.

Her designs "Decorating with Love" are being sold all over the U.S.A. and the National Home Fashions League made her, in 1981, "Woman of Achievement."

She is unique in that she was one and two in the Dalton list of Best Sellers, and one week had four books in the top twenty.

Barbara Cartland's book *Getting Older, Growing Younger* has been published in Great Britain and the U.S.A. and her fifth cookery book, *The Romance of Food*, is now being used by the House of Commons.

In 1984 she received at Kennedy Airport

America's Bishop Wright Air Industry Award for her contribution to the development of aviation. In 1931 she and two R.A.F. Officers thought of, and carried, the first aeroplane-towed glider airmail.

During the War she was Chief Lady Welfare Officer in Bedfordshire looking after 20,000 Service men and women. She thought of having a pool of Wedding Dresses at the War Office so a Service Bride could hire a gown for the day.

She bought 1,000 gowns without coupons for the A.T.S., the W.A.A.F.'s and the W.R.E.N.S. In 1945 Barbara Cartland received the Certificate of Merit from Eastern Command.

In 1964 Barbara Cartland founded the National Association for Health of which she is the President, as a front for all the Health Stores and for any product made as alternative medicine.

This is now a £300,000 turnover a year, with one third going in export.

In January 1988 she received "La Médaille de Vermeil de la Ville de Paris." This is the highest award to be given in France by the City of Paris. She has sold 25 million books in France.

In March 1988 Barbara Cartland was asked by the Indian Government to open their Health Resort outside Delhi. This is almost the largest Health Resort in the world.

Barbara Cartland was received with great enthusiasm by her fans, who fêted her at a reception in the City and she received the gift of an embossed plate from the Government.